P9-BHZ-594

To
Whitney from
Beware the Men
in the Woods!.

Love
Therese Brenelven
5/08

The Man

in the

Woods

By

Theresa J. Gonsalves

ISBN: 978-0-9762347-2-2
Hardcover – Limited Edition

Printing by:
RJ Communications, LLC
51 East 42nd Street, Ste 1202
New York, NY 10017

Library of Congress Cataloging in publication data
Gonsalves, Theresa 1958
The Man in the Woods
Library of Congress Control Number: 2007909389

Edited by: Wycedra Stokes

Cover Artwork drawing by: Donald Frye, Jr.

Copyright© 2008 by Theresa J. Gonsalves

Published by TJG Management Services, Inc., Las Vegas, NV
All Publishing Rights

In loving memory of

Winnie Washington

1945-2006

Acknowledgements

A special thanks to the owners of JavaStix (www.javastix.com) for keeping my coffee from spilling every day! Maybe soon Starbucks and the Coffee Bean will get the message!

I would like to dedicate this book to my children Todd Love Ball Jr. and Mychal Vincent Paul Oliver.

I would also like to dedicate this book to my only sister, Rhonda Gonsalves-Clementine and my brothers, Donald R. Frye, Jr., Ramon G. Frye (deceased), Ronald S. Gonsalves, Anthony C. Gonsalves, Mark Gonsalves, Dana Gonsalves, Ronnie Chambers and Ronald Sadm. In spite of it all, *I am still your sister!*

Thank You....

Lorraine McCollin, Vera Barnes, Tesha Young, Cedra Stokes, Illiya Clark, Kim Coleman, Marlene Frye, Monique Frye, Lisa Stewart, Loretta Fonfield, Tiffany Rothe, Marlisa Moschella, Dionne Washington, Candi Ivins, Ebonie Ennis, Julie Marcoulier, Nadine Peters, Vivian Rutherford, Stephanie Williams and last but not least Maxine Walker – *I am amazed and in aw of all these wonderful strong women in my life who are in my corner, supporting me in all that I do! I love you ladies!*

A very special thank you to Ms. Jasmine Carter!

Foreword

During the writing of this novel, I pose the question:

Do you think that we are predisposed to becoming who we are by heredity, by our surroundings or by things that have happened to us in the past? Does past behavior predict future behavior?

While scores of people feel as my stepmother does: *"God did not predetermine anyone to become a child molester. Those are choices one makes to continue the cycle of abuse. I do not believe if one is molested they automatically become the molester. I feel it is the same thing with being homosexual. It is a choice …..Midge Gonsalves."* there are a great many others who feel the very opposite.

I invite you to conclude your own truths as we follow **The Man in the Woods** from before his birth through December, 2007.

Approximately seventy-five percent of this book is based on fact; the rest is speculative or imagined.

About the actual Man in the Woods

"When we were growing up Stephen was just different. He was scary." – Nadine Peters (childhood friend)

It's been said you never have to

apologize for your family.

Me ... sometimes I feel like

I have to apologize for mine.

Sit back, relax and read!

Prologue

Virginia Beach 1996

It was an unusually warm Sunday, March morning in 1996, in the many woods of Virginia Beach. Animals ran freely without fear of capture. Trees shadowed the sun but didn't make it any cooler.

A large primitive and decaying shack hid from the beauty of the abundant acreage on the Woodlawn Estate. Overgrown trees with wood rotting-fungus hovered around the house and over the roof. Shingles on the ground indicated leaks in the ceiling. Three termite ridden logs held up the foundation of the shack, the other log having been eaten through causing the shack to lean. There was no running water or electricity. The front door hung on one hinge. On the side of the shack sat a bike that looked like it had just come out of the trash.

Virginia Beach Special Victims Unit Detective Young shook his head in disbelief at the fact that anyone could possibly live in this place. Black bears, wolves, jackrabbits, rams and deer are often encountered in these parts, he thought to himself. On a nice day he imagined these woods could be considered lovely, dark and deep. He yawned. He was tired. He had barely made the trek through the woods. Why hadn't the FBI sent their own men he wondered? Some days he hated his job. This was one of them. Detective Young radioed his back up to make sure everyone was in place.

Stephen had heard the crackling of broken tree branches and twigs and the rustling of the old fallen autumn leaves as the officers approached. It wasn't the sound of his many cats running home or the sound of the animals in the woods. It was noticeably the sound of approaching foot steps. He glanced out of what he called a window but was merely a hole in the wall and spotted his visitors. Their clothes, their strut, their approach, clearly told him they were the police. They were looking for the boy.

Carlos Diaz was his latest victim. Carlos ran away just before he turned twelve years old. He had been with Stephen for over six months. Standing four and a half feet tall, Carlos had dark black hair with large curls and a brownish-orange hue skin tone, wide brown eyes and very thick bushy eyebrows. His beautiful smile still housed clean white teeth. He had been seeking shelter, but mainly love, when Stephen took him in.

Four months earlier Stephen had found Carlos looking for food in the parking lot of Joey's Hamburgers. Carlos hadn't eaten real food for almost three days. Stephen had a couple of dollars on him so he took Carlos into the restaurant and fed him. Afterwards, he told Carlos he could come and live with him. Carlos was excited when Stephen had taken him to his house in the woods where no one could find him. In Carlos' mind, Stephen had just saved his life.

"Who's out there?" Carlos asked him as he too had heard the approaching footsteps. Living in the woods with Stephen, had taught him to listen for sounds that didn't fit within the norm.

"It's the police. They've come to get you I'm sure." Stephen responded trying to restrain the apparent panic in his voice. Carlos tensed, his lips quivered and he wanted to cry. He did not want to go home.

"Go run and hide in the closet," Stephen ordered hoping the corroded closet door would actually conceal the boy. He felt trapped. There was really no place the boy could hide.

"My time is up," Stephen thought to himself, "but I damn sure won't let them take me alive." Yes, dramatic, he thought but he had no desire to go back to jail.

Carlos had played throughout the entire shack and its outside surroundings and instead of going to the closet as instructed, Carlos knew of a better hideout he had stumbled upon. He didn't want to leave with the police. He didn't want to go back home. As long as he did what Stephen asked of him, he got love in return. Sometimes he didn't like the fondling and sex acts he had to endure. But it was sure better than having to do it with his stepfather just to please his mother as she watched.

Stephen took care of him in every other way also. His mom and step-dad barely fed him. His real dad was killed during a convenience store robbery, saving a woman in the line of fire. Carlos was proud of his dad. He had died a hero and that is what he will always remember. He missed him a lot.

Carlos scurried into one of the bleak bedrooms he shared with Stephen. Their bed, which wasn't much of one, consisted of a blood stained box spring they found on the side of a road that must have been on its way to a dumpster.

They carried it home together and placed it on the tattered wooden floor. It was the first furniture piece they had gotten together. Carlos lifted the box spring then lifted some floor boards that were joined together to form a small make shift door. He swiftly crept under the old trap door that led him to a crawl space just big enough for him to fit in. He huddled quietly and kept very still. He was afraid to even breathe once he heard voices inside their home. His wide eyes cased the small enclosed space. He saw spider webs, old candle drippings and what appeared to be old corn cobs, evidence of past lives having hid there long ago.

He closed his eyes, "I wonder if anyone ever died in here," he thought. Carlos was shaking with fear. He was determined not to succumb to it. A single tear slid down his cheek.

As Officer Johnson stood to the side, his right hand on his gun, Detective Young knocked, pushed the crooked door ajar and called out to Stephen just as Stephen was walking toward the door. "Mr. Gonsalves, are you in here?"
"Who are you?" Stephen questioned.
"I am Detective Young. Are you Stephen Gonsalves?" he asked showing his badge.

"Yeah," Stephen responded in a tone that asked "what do you want?"

"We're from Virginia Beach Special Victim Unit. We have reason to believe you are harboring a runaway boy named Carlos Diaz."

"Who? What? What are you talking about?" he answered astonishingly. May as well try to play it off, he snickered to himself.

"Carlos Diaz? Hispanic kid, about twelve years old. A runaway...We have permission from the property owner to search the premises," Detective Young said annoyed, pushing himself past Stephen and motioning for two back up officers to assist with the search. As he passed by Stephen, Detective Young inhaled the strong stench of his body odor. His face scrunched, his eyes flinched. It surely wasn't a pleasant aroma.

"Go ahead and search all you want. No one else is here. The only other thing here is what's left of my cats. The animals have been catching them and eating them," Stephen said sadly. They hesitated for a moment. They didn't know what to make of his comment. Was he trying to stall them?

The walls, ridden with holes, allowed you to see the entire contents of the shack from one room but the officers knew they still had to walk through the separate areas. They saw burnt candles; newspaper the officers assumed Stephen used for wiping his ass. An old cooler held a gallon of open water that was covered with aluminum foil. There was no ice. Cat food sat on carton pieces in what were the remains of the kitchen. The kitchen housed a small round table with rusted legs. The veneer wood that once covered it was now in pieces. Tuna cans, two white long candles, a large loaf of bakery bread, some playing cards and two plastic forks were strewn atop it.

In the bedroom they spotted the filthy urine stained box spring that was on the floor. Officer Johnson kicked the box spring to the other side of the room but with the decrepit wooden floors all three of the officers failed to notice the trap door opening. The quick glance of the naked eye wouldn't notice it.

The officers joined each other in the front of the shack. Stephen was outside the door as one officer kept watch on him.

"Hmm…" said Officer Johnson, "There doesn't seem to be any sign of any kid living here or having lived here. Maybe the parents just figured this man for the perp because he is living in the woods and is kind of strange. Who knows? It's your call Detective Young, should we haul him in?"

"Well, you're right. There are no visible signs of Carlos or any kids being here for that matter. So let's head out."

"It appears we have the wrong location, wrong man, Mr. Gonsalves. Sorry for the inconvenience," Detective Young stated as he and the four officers walked out of the shack.

"We'll watch him at his job for a few days," Young stated.

"This weirdo has a job?!!" Johnson responded incredulously.

"Yup, he sure does. Works at the city college. It's strange. Being that he's Black though, he really doesn't fit the profile of a pedophile. Wonder why he lives out here?"

"Must be some dumb ass Black man wanting to live like his ancestors use to live!" laughed an amused Officer Johnson. The others joined in his laughter.

Stephen had heard the smart ass comment made by Officer Johnson as he wondered where in the hell Carlos was hiding. He waited anxiously until they were no longer in view and then he went running through the shack yelling for Carlos. "They're gone Carlos. Where are you?" Stephen heard the sound of the creaking floor boards coming from their bedroom and ran in to see Carlos rising from the floor under the box spring.

He grabbed Carlos lifting him up and out from under the box spring and placed a firm kiss on his mouth, hugging him and holding him tightly in his arms.

"I was hiding under the floor daddy Stephen," he sniveled. Carlos loved calling him daddy, "I found this hiding place a while ago."

Stephen laughed aloud …"Oh yeah, I forgot these *were* slave quarters at one time. Lots of places like this in Virginia. Stupid ass police didn't do their homework."

"Yeah," Stephen said his laugh now a sinister one as he thought back to Officer Johnsons' racist joke, "I can keep you a little while longer."

Carlos smiled and hugged daddy Stephen happily because right now he wanted nothing more but to be where he was, with the man he now called daddy, with the man he lived with in the woods. When he was with Stephen he felt like a little young kid again.

After the episode with the police, Stephen felt that someone in his family should know what was going on in his life just in case he got caught. He wasn't going to go to prison for this. He would die first. He called his Aunt Tiny.

Rayetta Howard was his mothers' sister. All of the family called her Tiny. He considered her a replacement mom when his real mother died on March 11, 1993. He felt his sister Theresa should have taken their mothers' place, but Theresa had found that hilarious, yet she knew her brothers were serious. "All of us are over thirty!" she had exclaimed to Donald and Stephen, "You need to be responsible for your damn selves."

Aunt Tiny hadn't quite been prepared for what she heard, yet then again, who would be. Here was her nephew, whom she had given the nickname of *Tootie* at birth, telling her he was in love with a little boy and that the police and FBI were after him for kidnapping.

Aunt Tiny didn't know what to do with the information. She didn't want to turn him in, but she had to tell someone. As the thought ran through her mind her phone rang. Ironically, it was Stephen's sister Theresa. Instantly Aunt Tiny had her answer. This would lift the burden off of her. She didn't want the sole responsibility of knowing her nephew was a child molester.

"You need to talk to your brother," she told Theresa. "He is in love with some little boy that he kidnapped and the FBI is after him," Tiny informed her.

"What?!" Theresa exclaimed, clearly stunned "I talk to him almost every week. He didn't tell me any of that. I'll ask him about it though. Was he serious? No way. I know he's crazy but that sounds ridiculous." She was in disbelief.

But Theresa's surprise was short lived when she called Stephen that evening.

"Stephen, what is this Aunt Tiny is telling me about your being in love with some little boy and kidnapping him?"

"Oh. There was no kidnapping. But I can't talk about it over the phone, it might be tapped. But I love him Theresa. You just don't understand. I love him. I'll tell you all about it one day."

She was shocked at what she heard, but he refused to discuss it again in further conversations.

About three months later all conversation came to a halt. Stephen had gone to jail for stealing a steak and some cat food from the nearby Stop & Shop and the subject was pushed to the back of her mind when she received a phone call telling her that her youngest brother Donald had just stabbed their brother Ramon in the heart, killing him.

It was July 31, 1996.

Las Vegas, NV (October 2005)

Theresa felt the spasms in her stomach, while the taste of hot bile rose in her throat, as she tried to put the phone back in its cradle. The phone fell to the floor as she bent over into the small black trash can that sat by the desk in her office and began heaving uncontrollably. Along with the vomiting came uncontainable tears. She had remained composed throughout the conversation as she listened incredulously to what she was hearing. Her brother had just revealed to her that he had been molesting little boys for over twenty-five years.

"Ramon and Donald knew. Ask Donald, he'll tell you," he told her referring to their murderous, crack addicted youngest brother.

Gathering her poise, the horrid taste of vomit coating her throat, she sat back as tears continued to roll down her cheeks. Her mind was reeling with questions. "What the fuck was wrong with him? Had he been predisposed to this shit … molesting kids? Or did something snap in his brain when he was hit by the police car on its way to a crime scene when he was five. Maybe, just maybe, his brain was damaged when he banged his head against the wall for hours on end night after night after night before he would fall asleep or when he didn't get his way," she thought.

She sat pondering ways to turn him in. What other choice did she have? It was the boding evil, yet gentle, way he responded she recalled, when she asked, "What do you get out of messing with little boys?"

"They just feel so nice and soft and cuddly Theresa," he answered. His voice was dreamlike.

"How many of them were there?" she questioned not really wanting to hear a number.

"A lot ... I had me a ball, Theresa. Yeah, I had me a ball," Stephen recollected, his tone salivating the taste of his actions.

"How old were they?"

"From six to thirteen."

"Are you still doing it?"

"I was until Michael Jackson got caught. The first time he got caught, I figured I could keep doing it, but the second time I figured he had to stop now, so I better watch out too."

Stephen was her brother. She was still skeptical of his guilt, yet it was his voice on the other end of the line telling her this horrid information. She was hearing these words from his very own mouth. Theresa was torn between leaving him in his small little world as he made it and turning him in.

Then very hesitantly she asked him, *"Did you kill any of them?"* Theresa shuddered, feeling a chill run down her spine as she waited for his response. It never came. The call disconnected. She had no way of calling him back.

And suddenly her brother had become one to be very afraid of; more afraid than she could ever imagine.

14

He was now the boogey man who coveted the minds of the young. He was the Michael Meyers from the movies that scared us on Halloween nights. He was the Freddie Kruger who crept into our dreams. But in reality, he was now whom she identified as ... *the Man in the Woods!*

Theresa reflected over several thoughts as to what she should do. But mostly she wondered why. "Why did he end up this way? Why does a serial killer kill? Why does a child predator molest?"

She hated the comparison he had made to Michael Jackson. When she was with Michael Jackson at his apartment in New York in 1976, long before he was accused of being a child molester, she had bought him a book entitled, 'Somewhere a Child is Crying'. She had read it before giving it to him.

It gave her great insight as to why he loved and wanted to protect children so much. They each held back sniffles as they discussed the book and stories they heard that related to children being hurt.

It saddened her that Michael Jackson's desire to protect the children was turned into something so sick by the media. It saddened her even more that she almost had bought into the belief herself.

Now, her heart shaken, she had to confront this repulsion in her own family, her own brother. Her mind was swirling as she started reliving the memories of their lives.

Had it really been right there in front of her face? Of course it had. She had always been afraid of him. She had often questioned what he had done that made their mother leave him out of her will.

"What did you do to mummy?" she asked during their next conversation. She had to know the extent of his damage. She had to keep digging. She was adamant about finding out.

Stephen became very, very quiet. He just held the phone.

"What did you do to mummy?" she asked again her tone demanding a response.

"I didn't do anything to her," he lied as his mind flashed back to *that* night. She couldn't see through the phone, but she could visualize a smug annoyed look on his face. "Why would you ask me that?"

"Because she told me she was afraid of you," Theresa answered softly and sadly as she again speculated what he could have possibly put their mother through.

"Everyone is scared of me," he replied calmly.

"Yeah, well your own mother shouldn't be...." Theresa said her words fading away as the phone call once again disconnected. He was using one of the calling cards she had sent him. He didn't call back. She would again have to wait for him to call.

Theresa still couldn't find any answers within her soul as she reminisced about their childhood. But she wanted to know; no, she needed to know why. What made him this way? "Hmm ... other than an increased risk of high blood pressure common among Blacks of Cape Verdean ancestry, we don't really suffer any recognizable diseases or illnesses specific to *us*," she thought desperately reaching.

But ... ahh, yes there is always the *'but'*! Could our ancestry have given us a lineage of child molesters, rapist or murderers?

Psychiatrists tell us that becoming murderers, rapist or child molesters is something one is predisposed to. Are

17

these so called great psychiatrists of today correct? Are we predisposed to becoming who we are? Good or bad?

Theresa wanted to know as she wondered what other people would think.

"I have to search for the answer," she said aloud to herself, "but first there is one other thing I really must do." She picked up the telephone and called the Virginia Beach Police Department. "I want to report a child molester in the area."

"We will forward the message to the Special Victims Unit," the female officer told her after taking her name and cell phone number. Theresa thought of the television show Law & Order SVU when she said that and she let out a slight chuckle as the theme song played in her mind. It was one of her favorite shows. Her mind began to wander aimlessly with thoughts about their lives until the telephone rang, startling her.

It was Virginia Beach's Special Victims Unit.

"He (Carlos) wasn't the best one, but he was one of my favorites. There were way better ones than him. He was just so soft and cuddly Theresa. I like Hispanic looking ones better." – Stephen, aka the Man in the Woods

Chapter One

...the beginning, late 1930's
Cape Verde Islands

Her body swayed limply under the grip of his strong weathered hands strangling her tiny neck as life eased slowly out of her. The silence of the oceans edge echoed the sound of the snapping of her neck breaking so easily. She could no longer gasp for breath. You could barely see the rise and fall of her chest. Her long dark brown hair flowed beautifully with light curls falling softly down the side of her face. Cherene ...she was the daughter of a white Portuguese settler. She had unusual green eyes that matched the coral reef within the ocean water; she was small, very thin, weighing only sixty-five pounds.

Joseph watched her face as she took her last breath. He smiled with satisfaction after having ravished her small childish body. This ... *he* called making love. She was only twelve years old, the age when most little girls began having their first crush. She wasn't as easy as he had thought she would be. The others had given in so quickly.

He hadn't intended to kill her but he had always wanted to know what killing felt like and this was an opportune time.

Joseph Gonsalves was five feet ten inches tall. He was the tallest of the Gonsalves boys who spawned from the Cape Verde Island of Sao Vicente by way of Portugal. He had bushy eyebrows that shadowed squinty eyes. Add in what appeared to be the shadow of a new mustache and he looked more of a Puerto Rican descent instead.

He was just coming from a traditional Cape Verdean *Batuque Wedding Ceremony*. He had gotten horny as he watched the young girls perform the customary ritual dance afterward. They were nimble, they were sensual but they were just ten to twelve years old. Yet they stirred sexual feelings in him. Feelings that made him experience a sense of being out of control. As they danced, the young girls closed their eyes and held their little hands in front of their small faces in a gesture of wanting to be seen and appreciated while still intending to preserve their chastity and bashfulness.

With Cherene caught up in the mystery of love and marriage, it was easy for Joseph to entice her to follow him. She fantasized that perhaps he may be the boy of her dreams. She smiled as he held her hand and walked her to an isolated part of Sao Vicente's rocky beach. But her smiles and dreams quickly faded as she realized the dangerous mistake she had just made. This boy was no fantasy. This boy was *the* rapist of Sao Vicente Island.

Joseph thought back to how surprised she had been. Each girl would look at him adoringly at first until they realized he was the *'man'* the islanders were warning the young girls about. No one could possibly imagine he was just a kid himself. He thought back to how smooth Cherene had felt and how tight her vagina was. He closed his eyes to relive those recent moments. He instantly loved her in his own special way as he did them all. But for some reason she was more extraordinary than the others.

He relaxed his grip on her neck as small drops of blood dripped down the side of her mouth. He kissed her mouth tasting the blood. He savored her essence for at least five minutes. She smelled of a sweet scent like that of the purple Angel Face Rose and then lied her body down into the water. Food for the ocean prey, he offered. It was September, the month when the islands of Cape Verde got

21

most of its rain. If there is anything left of her after the sea urchins ate away at her, it would get washed away.

That was his last conquest in the Cape Verde Islands. He was heading to the United States with his three brothers, Ronald, Leslie and Carl along with their mother Olivia and their father Antonio Gonsalves.

It was 1946 when the Gonsalves family arrived in Boston, Massachusetts.

Joseph Gonsalves was just thirteen years old.

Chapter Two

Rose Street (mid 1940's)

The south end of Boston in the mid 1940's housed a variety of Black and Cape Verdean families. The era can detail the poverty of the time yet still in the mid 1940's, there was a lot going on, on Rose Street in the south end side of Boston, Massachusetts.

Several rows of three story apartment buildings housed at least six families and those families consisted of a number of unruly teenagers that filled the streets. It was a street filled with block parties, gambling, gang fights and sex.

Rosetta Bonds, a shy young teenager, stood out from the other girls on Rose Street. Standing only five feet two inches tall, she was very pretty and petite. At fifteen she had the beauty and aura of the short haired Dorothy Dandridge, the actress.

Rosetta was the middle child of three siblings, right in the middle of her sister Rayetta and her brother Harold. Their father had been attacked and robbed during a snowstorm and left for dead but a passerby found him unconscious in the snow and instead he was left with two frost bitten hands. When he was released from the hospital, Essie, their mother, felt he was a useless invalid and didn't desire to take care of him. Instead she put him out. When he left, it was as if he had simply disappeared off the face of the earth. Rosetta felt his abandonment. She was further dismayed when her brother Harold left and joined the army. There were no longer any men in her life.

Owning up to the theory that the middle child is always the one who suffers, Rosetta constantly vied for Essie's attention. Essie was an alcoholic and Rosetta was constantly cleaning up bouts of throw-up when her mother would go out binge drinking.

Essie's constant bedwetting gave their home a consistently urinous scent. No matter how hard Rosetta tried to please Essie, Essie never took notice. When she couldn't get love from her mother, it was no wonder, at the age of fifteen, Rosetta sought out love on Rose Street.

Ronald Gonsalves lived on the same street two buildings down. The matriarch of the Gonsalves family was Olivia Gonsalves formerly Olivia Day. All the girls in the neighborhood, at their school and no matter where they went, were fascinated with the Gonsalves boys and the fact that they were Cape Verdean. They were warm yellow skin toned brothers with fine black hair and all the girls fantasized about having their babies.

Their father Antonio Gonsalves had decided to return to his original Portugal roots. The transition to the United States had made him solemn and depressed and he took it out on his wife and kids. He missed his surroundings no matter how barren they may have been.

He needed the calmness of the ocean waters, the fishing and the intense darkness of the nights that existed in Sao Vicente.

Olivia had decided she and her boys would stay. She easily adapted to the United States and had fallen in love with it. Boston was now her home. She had made many friends whom she entertained with card games and Pokeno.

Olivia was older than the other mothers who had children of the same ages. Most of the women her age were already grandmothers. She had given birth to her last child at the age of 40. She had always hoped for a daughter nevertheless ended up with four sons. Her mother had been a proud woman of German and African descent with Indian like long dark black hair that she often kept in a bun. It was said that she was so beautiful men often fought over her. When one man loved her so much and couldn't have her, he instead killed her so no one else would either.

The Gonsalves boys were an unruly group of young men. They were considered dangerous along with their friends Clayton and Tommy who also lived on Rose Street. Rumor had it that they were notorious for committing gang rapes and possibly murders. Most people believed it was true because the oldest Gonsalves boy, Joseph, at the age of twenty was already in jail for killing a girl he had also raped. The small story appeared in the back page of the Boston Record Newspaper Negro section. The newspaper felt no need to glamorize anything that had to do with Negroes.

"Joseph Gonsalves, age 20, was arrested for the rape and second degree murder of twelve year old Barbara Winters. He was sentenced to sixteen years in Norfolk prison."

Barbara Winters had only been twelve years old. But since she was a little colored girl, the punishment wasn't as severe.

There had been several young children molested in the neighborhood and that number dwindled once Joseph went off to prison. The correlation was easily perceived but no one would dare make mention of it. It was safer to keep quiet when it came to the Gonsalves boys. Olivia seldom spoke of Joseph once he was put away.

Ronald Gonsalves had eyed Rosetta often. She always looked cute with her small waistline and she often wore her hair in curls. He loved when she wore her hair back off her face because it showed the gracefulness of her silhouette. She was the one girl who hadn't tried to chase him.

Rosetta kept her eyes on him closely too. She knew he was a womanizer and all the girls loved him. He was a short boy, just two inches taller than she was. She would be taller than him in heels, she laughed to herself, but still, he was the most handsome boy she had ever seen. His stylish and polished conk, also known as a *do*, made him look even finer. She knew he wanted her. She also knew the way to get him was to make him come after *her*.

And that he did. He did the traditional dating with Rosetta. He took her to the movies. He actually waited to walk her home from school. He did all the right things until she decided she was ready to become his.

Rosetta was a virgin when she lay down to give herself to Ronald. She was just fifteen years old. She had heard stories, like when her cherry was broken, there would be a lot of bleeding and pain. Yet she didn't feel any pain. She just felt like she was being loved. Something she didn't feel she was getting at home. But naivety led them quickly down a different path as sadly, within two months, Rosetta was pregnant. She had just turned sixteen years old.

Ronald wasn't ecstatic, but accepting of it. Ronald stopped having sex with her. He didn't want to hurt the baby he had said.

However, Rosetta suspected otherwise and it didn't take her long to find her suspicions were true when she followed him from work one afternoon and found out that he was seeing another girl. After school Ronald worked putting together the newspapers for the Boston Record.

Ronald got off work at just about the same time every day and Rosetta knew the route he normally took. When he got off the train at Dover Street Station, Rosetta, who laid in waiting, began following him to see what was taking him so long to make his way home. She was livid when she found him knocking on the door of Juanita Chambers.

Juanita lived in the Cathedral Projects. Ronald had to walk down either Washington Street or Harrison Avenue and pass the Projects to get to Rose Street. While Ronald truly loved Rosetta, she was too straight laced for him. Juanita offered an element of danger.

Rosetta waited outside the apartment for a half an hour before knocking on the door. She was screaming and yelling for Ronald as she knocked. Rosetta's anger was triple fold when she confronted Juanita and they stood eye to eye, *both* with small protruding stomachs. Rosetta sensed instantly that the baby in Juanita's belly was Ronald's child. Rosetta's breathing intensified, her small fist clenched, her eyes bulged as rage set in and then suddenly without warning, she let out a growling yell as she grabbed Juanita by the hair and swung her to the ground. She was about to stomp on her stomach when Ronald suddenly appeared and grabbed her away. He had quickly run and hid when he saw Rosetta approaching Juanita's door.

"You keep that crazy bitch away from me Ronnie!" Juanita yelled at him, now showing bravery since he showed up.

"I will kill you and that kid!" Rosetta yelled back as she tried to escape his hold and go after her.

"Let's go!" Ronald yelled dragging Rosetta, being sure not to hurt her.

He had almost been true to his words. He stopped making love with Rosetta, because at seventeen, he was just young and naïve enough to believe that if he put his penis in hard enough, she would miscarry. He simply figured all the pummeling up and down could cause that. He tried it with Juanita constantly, almost robotically and forcefully until he finally realized he was going to be stuck with two kids.

Rosetta gave birth in April 1954 to a baby boy they named Anthony Curtis after Ronald's dad, who left them for the desires of Sao Vicente.

Juanita gave birth in May, 1954 to a baby boy she named after Ronald just to spite Rosetta. But alas, Rosetta had what she thought was the last laugh when Ronald dumped Juanita and said he wanted to be with only her.

With two boys born at the same time, Ronald had no choice but to quit school to get a full time job. He found a job at the ship yard Boston Army Based Pier in South Boston as a shipper. He loaded and unloaded the vessels. He was lucky to have gotten the job. He just did his job and invoked the waterfront rules, "Don't ask any questions. Don't answer any questions." So he never really knew what was actually being imported or exported. The bad part was getting to and from the job and having to go through South Boston and clusters of angry racist whites.

Rosetta was a sophomore in high school when she had to quit school as well. She found a job as a stitcher. She could work magic with any Singer Sewing Machine! They had no choice but to work to take care of their child. Olivia Gonsalves however, was a welcomed help when she took on a lot of the responsibility.

Chapter Three

Galena Street

At eighteen Rosetta was pregnant again for the second time. They had moved into their own place on Galena Street in Roxbury. They occupied a small two bedroom of a duplex house. Rosetta's best friend Carol Thatcher had moved into the unit next to them. She too had been trapped with pregnancy at an early stage of their lives. They were both naïve to love, sex and apparently men.

Ronald was a good provider but he still constantly snuck around with plenty of other women. At this point, most days Rosetta was simply indifferent towards it. He had also taken on another job because the work on the waterfront was slow. He began working at Wayne's Shoe factory where he was an order puller. He worked hard to take care of their small growing family ... "and his other kid."

There were plenty of days when Ronald simply felt tied down and caged in. And now he was about to have a third child. Although he felt trapped in this situation, he still kept living his life his own way. He continued hanging out with his friends and doing whatever it was he wanted to do.

Every weekend Ronald and his boys would meet at one of their houses to see what they could get in to.

It was on one of those weekend nights that Rosetta was awakened by the noise coming from the front room of her home. Unaware that they had just come in, she was annoyed as their loud voices carried into her bedroom as the regular crew, Ronald, his brothers and their buddy Clayton played their usual poker game. Their pal Tommy had decided to stay home that night.

They didn't hear Rosetta as she came out of the bedroom and walked into the kitchen to get some ice water. She had just been awakened from a restless pregnant sleep. Her mouth was extremely dry. She desperately needed something to drink.

As she put the glass of water to her mouth, she began to listen intently as she thought it weird that they were all breathing heavily as if they were out of breath. Their words came across in loud, clear whispers.

"Oh man, I could have shot my rocks off two times if the bitch's knees hadn't buckled," Clayton said proudly and disturbingly.

"Who tied her to that damn pole with that extension cord? Her wrists were bleeding!" said Carl Gonsalves who never participated in these gang rapes, but always stood watch; which in essence made him just as guilty.

"Aww, so what man. Are you having a bleeding heart over that?"

"Yeah man Carl, you know she wanted it. They always do."

"That was pretty risky to do at Dudley Station."

Dudley station was the main train and bus terminal that sat right in the middle of the predominantly Black Roxbury neighborhood. It was a wide open station and anyone driving by could see inside. The buses and trains normally stopped running by two a.m.

"Yeah man, except that girl was prime! She was worth the risk!"

There was no regret, no remorse, just conquerors' boasting.

Rosetta stood paralyzed by what she had heard until the conversation turned back to their poker game. Her hands were shaking. She almost dropped her glass. She removed her slippers and quietly crept back to her bedroom.

Rosetta had also heard the rumors about their gang rapes; she simply chose not to believe them. Ronald had always been so gentle with her. Suddenly her thoughts were interrupted as she felt the baby kick very hard inside her stomach and then stiffen itself up. Extreme nausea consumed her. She ran to the bathroom, quickly but quietly.

Chapter Four

A Molester is born

The pregnancy was filled with constant pain but the delivery itself during the evening of November 3, 1956 was without pain. He did not emerge crying, but with sullen staring wide eyes. After Rosetta gave birth to Stephen, she wrapped him in a baby blue receiving blanket she had received from the unwanted baby shower. She hadn't really looked at his face. She couldn't explain it to herself let alone anyone else. All she knew was that she could not take this child home with her. She had the traditional white flowered hospital gown on under an ankle length beige trench coat so no one realized she was a patient as she walked through the dungeon of Boston City Hospital and right out the front door with her newborn child in her arms.

It was a chilly night, but Rosetta didn't feel the cold as she walked down Mass Ave in a trance like state. She knew exactly where she was heading. She was like a zombie. The walk was long, about twenty minutes, but unmemorable to her.

When she arrived on the bridge of Boston's Charles River that connected Boston and Cambridge, Massachusetts, she simply stood there contemplating what she was about to do. The night was very calming to her. Thugs, yuppies with their dogs and various strangers walked by but barely noticed her. Something was always happening on the bridge but when it happened people didn't always see it nor accept it.

She looked out at the water and up at the sky. She had a silent talk with God. She wasn't very good in the religion department. They were Catholics in name only.

Finally she felt it was time to do what she had gone there to do. He would die on impact and just go under. He wouldn't suffer long.

She held her new born son over the bridges barrier and began saying a prayer and as she was about to drop him, Carl Gonsalves, the youngest of the Gonsalves boys, appeared seemingly out of no where.

"You don't have to do that," he spoke calmly. Carl was her brother in law. He had always liked Rosetta and had been on his way to visit her and to see his new nephew when he spotted her walking out of the hospital with the baby and

decided to follow her. She had just had the baby hours ago and he knew it was too soon for her to be released. He had called out to her several times but she didn't seem to hear him.

"Just give him to me."

He wasn't sure she had heard him, "Rosetta ...give me the baby" he demanded.

He reached out and took the baby from her. He could feel her shaking heavily. There was no emotion, just a blank stare. He put his arm around her shoulder while holding Stephen in the other. To her it felt like a warm blanket. "Don't worry," he told her, "I'll take care of everything."

Rosetta tried hard to understand why she felt such fear of this baby. Carl discussed the incident with his brother Ronnie. They decided for now that baby Stephen would be better off with their mother Olivia instead. So when he was released from the hospital, Carl delivered the baby to its grandmother.

Chapter Five

After giving birth to Stephen, Rosetta stayed in a constant daze. She was despondent. She simply was going through the motions of life. She played with Anthony every day. She continued working at her sewing job. At least that was something she was very good at and enjoyed. Sometimes a smile would come to her face as she fantasized about designing and modeling her own clothing line. When she didn't see that dream as a real possibility, she began to feel like a prisoner in her own home.

Ronald handled most of their financial affairs and only gave her enough money for the bare necessities and a small allowance. "Yet," she pouted, "he always had money for his poker games and whatever else he wanted to do."

So Rosetta began demanding at least the responsibility of handling their finances. Ronald decided to try to make her happy by giving her that control. He had noticed her discouraged state since the birth of Stephen and wanted to help her in anyway he could. After all, he did truly love her.

But what a disaster it turned out to be. After just two months, he had to regain control when he found their electricity being shut off for the second time. She had been buying cookies, cupcakes and candy as a way to retreat back to being the little girl she never had the chance to really be; the little girl that she truly missed.

Too early in life, she had taken on the responsibility of a family. But in trying to do whatever it took to make her happy, Ronald proposed marriage and Rosetta accepted.

Ronald and Rosetta were wed on December 22, 1956, a little over one month after Stephen's birth. They were both just eighteen years old. They were still kids learning how to play house.

The wedding was small and simple. It was held at the Catholic Cathedral on Harrison Ave. Rosetta's best friend Carol Thatcher was her Maid of Honor.

Rosetta was indeed a beautiful bride. Her dress, hand sewn by Rosetta herself, was a calf length white sleeveless dress with three layers of satin and lace ruffles. A white lace matching shawl covered her shoulders. Her long dangling faux diamond earrings glittered like real ones. Her hair was simply bundled in curls. Her smile lit up the small cathedral church. She was marrying Ronald Gonsalves. He was the love of her life and her children's father.

For days after the ceremony, she was still on top of the world. But she still remained leery of her newest born child, Stephen.

On occasion, Rosetta would go to her mother-in-laws to visit Stephen, hoping one day to evoke some kind of feelings towards him. Her first son, Anthony, was growing up fine and she loved him dearly. She couldn't understand the lack of affection she felt for baby Stephen.

Her mother in law, now Olivia Fisher was a strong woman. She was now fifty-eight years old and taking on this huge responsibility of her grandson. Olivia had sensed there was something wrong with Stephen. He never cried. He wasn't very responsive, but she loved and cared for him anyway. While she had raised four sons already, she felt a responsibility to her grandchildren.

Olivia's second husband, Irving Fisher, just sat quietly in his rocking chair and simply allowed her to do whatever she felt necessary. She made sure a home cooked meal was on the table for him every evening when he arrived from work.

After Antonio had returned to Sao Vicente, Olivia met Irving at a neighborhood dance. She married him to have a father for her four boys. But Irving was old and tired so the role he took on as a father was minimal at best as was his role of being a grandfather. Her sons didn't respect him as a stepfather but they loved him for caring for their mom.

Irving managed to bring comfort to Olivia. He loved the kids but felt too old to do more than that. While none of the kids knew of their real paternal grandfather, it was odd that they all called Irving by his first name, instead of grandpa. The children barely saw Irving out of his rocking chair.

Chapter Six

A little over a year after her marriage to Ronald, in early 1958, Rosetta found herself pregnant yet again. She would be turning twenty in July and already on her third child. She feigned happiness to the public eye. "Not again," she thought to herself, "I have already been able to self-abort two pregnancies. This damn rhythm method is useless and that damn Ronald never pulls out in time anyway."

Unfortunately for Rosetta, Ronald had noticed all the pregnancy symptoms this time and was excited about perhaps having a daughter to be daddy's little girl. She couldn't possibly try to self abort this time. "So here I go again," she thought. She felt truly exasperated.

Leaning over the bathtub now filled with discolored dirty water, as she scrubbed clothes against a shabby, light brown, old, wooden washboard, Rosetta was worn out. Small beads of perspiration trickled down the side of her face and her protruding seven month pregnant stomach was getting in the way when she was startled by a rude, loud knock on the door.

Ronald was in the bed asleep. He would have to get up within the next two hours to go to his night job. Their eldest son Anthony was in the living room playing with his green army toys and brown Lincoln logs. Anthony jumped up and ran to the door and opened it. Rosetta approached the living room as quickly as she could to quiet down the noisy visitor before they could awaken her husband.

Two White police officers, in full black uniform, stood tough and rigid in the doorway. Their intimidating looks scared Anthony and he ran and hid behind his mother.

"Can I help you?" Rosetta asked meekly, her eyebrows raised in surprise to find policemen at her door.

"Yes ma'am. We're looking for Ronald Gonsalves. Is he home?" they asked as they gently but deliberately pushed her aside making their way into her home.

Rosetta began shaking violently but tried to hold up a front for her son. "Yes he is here. What is this about?" she questioned fearfully.

"Where is he ma'am?" one of the officers' demanded.

Rosetta pointed to their bedroom. They pulled out their guns and walked into the bedroom. Rosetta gasped, putting her hands over her mouth, "Oh no...Oh my God," she sobbed.

Ronald was lying in a sound sleep wearing only a t-shirt and boxers. He was still working two jobs to provide for his family. He was awakened by the two police officers, kicking on the side of the bed, one holding a gun close to the back of his head.

"Mr. Gonsalves you are under arrest for the rape of Miss Angela Butler."

They grabbed his arms twisting them behind his back and handcuffed him. He was barely awake and had no opportunity to resist arrest. As they walked out the bedroom, Rosetta held Anthony back as he cried to the police officers, "Please don't take my daddy! Please don't take my daddy!"

Fighting to get away from his mother, Anthony kicked one of the officers as he walked by.

"You need to control your kid Mrs. Gonsalves. Apparently you couldn't control your husband. He is under arrest for rape!" the officer snapped viciously.

Rosetta didn't say a word as she watched the officers put her husband into the patrol car. She noticed a

small crowd had gathered. She slammed the door and went
back to washing clothes.

Chapter Seven

Two weeks later, as the dutiful wife, Rosetta sat through the court proceedings and listened to her husband get sentenced for participating in the gang raping of sixteen year old Angela Butler.

Angela had been a virgin. At a party, she had flirted with their buddy Clayton. Clayton immediately interpreted that as an invitation for sex and wanted to make sure he shared with his boys as they had done so many times before.

Clayton, Ronald and Tommy took her into the bathroom and each watched while the other took turns pulling a train on her, ignoring the blood, ignoring her weeping. A face cloth had been stuck in her mouth to stifle any loud cries. The thunderous music emitting from the party's record player helped to block out any sounds that may have come from the bathroom that evening. They had requested fast Motown tunes be played.

When they were finished with Angela they sent her friend Diane in the bathroom to get her. With satisfactory smirks on all of their faces, Clayton had told Diane, "Clean her up and get her the fuck out of here."

As Rosetta sat through the proceedings, she thought back to the night she had over heard them bragging about one of their conquests and she knew they were all guilty of this gang rape. Their defense was that she wanted it and felt ashamed afterwards. To them it was a game.

Now here she sat, alone seven months pregnant already with two kids. Rosetta did not want to continue to go through with this pregnancy, especially without her husband. But it was too late. Deep down Rosetta despised this unborn child already. "Would she feel the same about this baby as she did Stephen?" she wondered. "If I wasn't pregnant with this baby we would be able to have sex and he wouldn't be raping anyone," she wanted desperately to believe. He had promised her that he wouldn't cheat on her again but whenever she was pregnant he would not have sex with her as he still held that adolescent fear of hurting the baby. Rosetta blamed her unborn child.

She lay in bed later that evening knowing what she had to do. She couldn't have this baby. She couldn't give birth to another child that she wouldn't love. It would only remind her of what Ronald had done.

Their bedroom was small and crowded, fitting only a queen size bed and a long dresser drawer with a large mirror. Perfume bottles and Ronald's cologne covered the top of it. The room was painted a light blue and Rosetta had some extra flowered green and blue material from her seamstress job that she used to make the curtains that hung from the two windows that opened to the east side of the morning. The sunset often flooded the room. A basket of clothing that she had removed from the clothes line earlier that day sat at the edge of the bed waiting to be folded.

Rosetta went to the closet and pulled out a hanger. She twisted the hanger apart and rubbed it in alcohol that she had removed from the bathroom medicine cabinet. She had successfully done this before and no one had ever been the wiser. She did realize she had never been as far along as she was now. She watched herself in the mirror as she slowly took off the panties she was wearing under her nightgown. She looked at her stomach and rubbed her hands over it.

She placed an old brown towel on top of the sheet on her bed. She lied on top of the towel, pulled up her gown so that it wasn't in the way and held up her knees, her feet resting on the bed, her legs spread widely apart. Saying a prayer for forgiveness, she slowly stuck the hanger into her vagina up as far as she could go. The pain was instant and excruciating. She hadn't expected that. It hadn't been so painful before. She began to scream but she couldn't stop herself from sticking the hanger in a second time and still a third time. It was as if she were punishing herself. She felt blood, thick and sticky, and then the warmth of water bursting and draining down her thighs to her buttocks and on to the towel.

Labor pains began immediately with instant sharp cramping. Her vagina tightened shut to try to keep out the invading object and she again began to scream.

Her best friend Carol who lived right next door, wall to wall, heard the horrid screams and ran over to Rosetta's place, letting herself in to see what was going on. "Damn," she cried in terror, her eyes taking in the bedroom scenario as she cringed at the sight of the large amount of blood that was on the towel. "What the hell did you do

Rosetta? What the hell did you do?" She didn't know what else to do but get help.

Neither of them could afford a telephone. Carol sprinted down the street to the phone booth at the corner as fast as she could to call for help. It was free to dial zero for the operator.

"Oh, my God! Oh my God, please send help to 12 Galena Street. My friend is in labor. There is blood everywhere. She's not fully conscious!"

Carol ran back to the house and to her friend's side. "Rosetta what the hell did you do?" she questioned caringly. "What did you do?" She tried to be strong for her friend, but she couldn't stop the tears that trickled down her cheeks.

Carol squirmed at the sight of all the blood as she pried the hanger from Rosetta's hand and threw it under the bed along with the bloodied towel. Blood seeped onto the sheets. Carol made a mental note to be sure to come back and clean up later. She didn't know if what Rosetta had just done was a crime or not. What was obvious to Carol was that Rosetta was trying to kill this baby.

The gossip of self-abortion had often spread throughout the neighborhood. All of the girls had heard of different ways to do it but she had never known anyone to try it, especially so late in a pregnancy.

As Carol was about to run out to call for a cab, the ambulance finally arrived. Rosetta was in full labor. It was too soon. The baby probably wouldn't survive. The medical resources were limited for Black folks at that time. She had lost a lot of blood and Carol was beside herself with worry. She surely wasn't going to watch her friend die. Rosetta was in and out of consciousness.

Carol rode in the ambulance yelling at the driver "Get your ass moving." The hospital was just blocks away yet it seemed an eternity before the ambulance pulled into the emergency entrance.

Carol paced the hospital waiting room wondering who she should call. "Shit, her no good husband is in jail. Where was little Anthony? Where is her damn sister?" she wondered after trying to call her several times.

Finally, the doctor came out to talk to her. "Close call with this one," the doctor told her shaking her head knowingly but without conviction.

Dr. Annette Adair had seen too many deaths of women who tried to perform their own abortions. She had seen the deep puncture wounds in Rosetta's uterus and noticed healed wounds she assumed were from other actual closet abortions. She could tell the object Rosetta had used was a hanger. She shuddered at the thought of how that must have felt. She had treated other women who had tried to use a vacuum hose or even a tree branch. Dr. Adair knew she was in for a battle when she decided to join those who would fight for the day abortion would become a safe matter of choice.

"Go on in," Dr. Adair told her, "She will be asleep for a while. In case you're wondering, she has an underweight baby girl that we will have to keep for a little while." She tried to smile. What should have been a happy occasion truly was not.

Carol was sitting at her side when Rosetta awoke at 1:00 a.m. She looked at Rosetta and smiled.
"She's a preemie, but we can fatten her up. You have a little baby girl."

Rosetta closed her eyes choking back any emotional outbreak. She could still feel the affect of the drugs they had given her.

"I thought we were going to lose you," Carol said sadly, "you should be thankful you are still alive. I don't know what you were thinking."

It was the Monday before Thanksgiving, November 24th, 1958.

"I will try to be thankful for my daughter and thankful I didn't kill myself. I'll name my little girl Theresa after the Catholic saint. Maybe that will help her," Rosetta whispered to her friend.

They kept Theresa in the hospital until she weighed enough to go home and had recovered from her surgery. She had a strangulatory hernia which they had to surgically repair and she was born with a small hole in her tiny heart that would need to be monitored for a couple of years until it closed.

Chapter Eight

Still continuing to be the dutiful wife, Rosetta visited her husband at the prison every weekend. She brought little Theresa for a visit so he could see. He beamed with pride at the sight of his first daughter.

"You better hope no man does to her what you have done to me," she thought she had said to herself but actually had stated aloud. Ronald chose to ignore what he heard and enjoy the monumental moment of meeting his daughter.

The loneliness Rosetta felt with her husband in prison became extreme after awhile. Her baby girl, Lil T she called her, was six months old now, yet the joy of motherhood still evaded her. Yes, she went through the motions of being a good mother because it was what was expected. After all, she thought, this little thing can't survive on her own. Carol was helping her as much as she could but was now pregnant herself.

Rosetta was lucky that Olivia was still caring for her son Stephen and when Rosetta went to work as a stitcher during the day, Olivia would have all of the children.

But then came the day Rosetta met a suave and debonair young man named Donald Frye. He had the most amazing muscles she had ever seen. He had been a service man and sure looked good in uniform. Donald Frye was tall yet physically built with sandy brown unflawed skin. He had a small mustache under a pointed nose. His eyebrows were thick and spread evenly above small squinty eyes. Most of the women described him as dreamy and each of them looked at him that way.

He had completed his four year stretch as a soldier in the Army and was now taking it easy working as a clerk in the corner store down the street. All the kids loved Don Frye especially Anthony. They called him Uncle Don. He was the candy man. Because he himself was so fond of Don Frye, Anthony insisted on taking his mom into the store to meet him.

Their attraction to one another was instant and undeniable and against her solemn oath to be faithful to her husband. Yet still Rosetta began dating Donald Frye.

Immediately upon finding out, one of Ronald's boys went up to the jailhouse to visit Ronald and informed him that his wife was cheating on him. His anger was apparent upon hearing the news. There was nothing he could personally do so he instructed his boys to deal with it.

There was always something happening in the neighborhood and all of the shade drawn windows had eyes. Everyone knew that Rosetta was dating Don Frye. She was cheating on one of the Gonsalves'. Did she not care for that man's life the nosy neighbors had wondered as they gossiped amongst themselves as Don Frye day after day blatantly parked his car in front of Rosetta and Ronnie's home.

There were only three steps up to the front door to their place. On that day, Don Frye only made it to the first step before Carl, Leslie and Clayton grabbed him.

They threw him down on the ground and gave him the worse beating of his life, making sure to kick him in his face. Holding a knife to his neck, Clayton warned him, "Stay away from what isn't yours or the next time you're a dead man!" He pushed Don's head down hard on the concrete ground. The sound of his skull cracking echoed the silence of the night as they walked away leaving him bleeding on the sidewalk.

Rosetta watched from her living room window as did the neighbors. Everyone was too afraid to go out and stop them or call the police. Police never showed up to help them anyway, only to arrest.

As soon as the fellows were out of sight, Rosetta ran outside with Anthony to help Don. She called next door to Carol who came out to help her. They managed to get Don into his car, they locked the kids in the house and they hopped in his car and Carol sped to the hospital. Rosetta didn't know how to drive yet. They dropped him off at the hospital entrance, leaving his car there.

"Rosetta ... I'm okay. Don't forget, I was a soldier. I will be fine," he was able to mumble. "I love you."

She kissed him hastily then she and Carol ran the five blocks back to Galena Street as fast as they could to get back to the kids.

On Sunday Rosetta, still continuing to be the dutiful wife, went up to the prison to visit her husband. They had their normal casual banter. She told him what was going on in the neighborhood. Suddenly, while she was mid-sentence talking about their daughter and how feisty she was, he stopped her.

"I heard you had a boyfriend."

He saw the instant fear well in her eyes and could clearly hear the loudness of her quickening heart beat as she nervously tried to respond.

"It's okay," he told her, "I understand. But when I get out of here, you have to decide what you want to do."

She was caught off guard by his words. It was so matter of fact. "Was this his way of making amends for what he had done?" she wondered. She didn't deny nor confirm. Dumbfounded she left and decided not to visit again.

Don Frye did not take heed to the warnings. Bandaged and bruised he showed up at her home again just two days later. Rosetta, Carol and Tiny were sitting in her living room when he arrived.

"You must be crazy!" Tiny exclaimed shaking her head in disbelief.

"No. My father always told me, if you want something bad enough you just take the risk," he said as he tried to flash Rosetta a sexy smile while wincing with pain.

It was in that instance Rosetta Gonsalves fell head over heals in love with Donald Frye.

Chapter Nine

Just after Theresa's first birthday, Ronald was released from prison. Prior to his release, Olivia had a talk with Rosetta. Olivia had been the majority caregiver to Rosetta's three children. Although Rosetta worked by doing piece work at a nearby sewing factory, she couldn't have maintained much of a lifestyle on her own. Olivia was the sole provider of little Stephen, the child that Rosetta couldn't bare to be alone with. Olivia knew Rosetta was dating another man but she strongly suggested to Rosetta that she take her husband back.

Out of respect for Olivia but against her own feelings, she decided it was the right thing to do.

Rosetta still loved her husband but she couldn't forgive him for what he had done. While she had tried to block out what she had overheard, she couldn't block out the fact that he had gone to jail and confirmed to everyone that he and his boys had been responsible for numerous gang rapes. He denied actually raping Angela Butler although admitted he was simply guilty by just being there.

Nevertheless, Rosetta felt he went to jail for the ones he hadn't been caught for.

Rosetta hesitantly made love to her husband when he came home. She was just going through the motions. She went through several weeks of pretension, missing Don Frye more and more each day. When she couldn't stand not communicating with him any longer she hid in the bathroom and wrote him a note on a brown paper bag feeling it would be less conspicuous.

> *"Dear Don,*
>
> *I had to let you know that I miss you and I love you very much. I want to be with you and I know when the time is right we will be together. I will try to see you as soon as I can. Just remember that I love you. Rosetta."*

She took the letter, folded it up and gave it to her son Anthony who was now five.

"Anthony, I need you to go and give this to Don Frye."

"Okay Mom," he replied with a smile as he jumped up off the floor. Anthony liked Don Frye. He had been the one responsible for their meeting. Anthony hopped on his bike and headed down the street. Arriving at the end of Galena Street, about to make a turn onto Mass Ave, he screeched on his brakes as he ran straight into his dad, causing Anthony to fall off of his bike.

"Hey! Hey! Hey! Slow down. Where are you to going so fast?"

"Going to give this note to Don Frye," he responded with a child's innocence holding up the brown note.

"What? What note? Let me see it," his dad demanded angrily. Just hearing Don Frye's name infuriated him.

"No! Mom told me to only give it to Don Frye!"

"Boy, give it to me!" Ronald yelled grabbing his son.

"No, No, No," he shouted back actually trying to fight with his father.

Ronald held his son down and took the note.

"Pick up your bike and get home," Ronald ordered.

They walked quickly while Anthony cried unsure of what was going on. All he was doing was what his mother had asked him to do.

"Sit out here on the steps until I tell you to come in," Ronald firmly admonished his oldest son.

Ronald walked quietly through the front door, into the house, opening the letter as he crept inside. Rosetta was in the bedroom straightening up. She was smiling as she thought by now Don must have received her letter.

Disbelief and rage welled up from deep inside Ronald as he read the words his wife was writing to another man. He stormed into their bedroom.

"I love you and I miss you!" he hollered at the top of his lungs waiving the note in the air, intending to frighten her. "And you had the nerve to have my son delivering this bullshit!"

Rosetta jumped. Her eyes widened with fear. She backed up.

"How dare you?" he yelled pushing her. She cowered back into a corner as he reached over and grabbed her by her neck with both his hands, lifting her off the ground strangling her. "Please Ronald no..." she gasped feeling her life being choked out of her. "Please no..." she could hardly get out the words.

Ronald couldn't hear her cries. Fury had seized his mind. He applied more pressure on his grip as the words kept jumping off the scribbled brown page into his face.

Then a vision of prison flashed before him. He released the pressure of his hands around her neck and dropped her on the bed. She fell like a rag doll, gulping for every bit of air that surrounded her. She had been fifteen seconds away from death.

As she laid there struggling to regain her breath, coughing, Ronald got her a wet cloth and some cold water. He dragged his suitcase out of the closet and started packing his clothes.

Afterwards, he sat there dismayed just looking at her. He was disgusted with himself and Rosetta. He had almost killed his wife. It was time to leave.

When she was able to sit up on her own, Ronald looked her directly in her eyes, "I'm sorry." His voice was filled with remorse. She knew he meant it as he turned around and walked out the door without another word.

She was free.

Chapter Ten

Ronald moved into the 224 Lamartine Street home in Jamaica Plain where Olivia and Irving had moved with Stephen. They had an extra bedroom which normally acted as Theresa's bedroom because she was there every weekend and most summers.

Stephen was still a quiet kid. He slept a lot and didn't interact with other children much until he met the little red headed white boy Jackie that lived in the house down the side of the alley.

Olivia had befriended Jackie's mother Joannie, who came over to the house from time to time.

Olivia was happy that Stephen had some semblance of a friendship. She noticed that he and Jackie played but seldom spoke. When he wasn't playing with Jackie, she would often find Stephen sitting in the closet playing with the sun rays that would shine through the windows.

He also was attached to her cat Red. Red was a big mean alley cat. When Theresa came over Red had to be locked in the bedroom. This made Stephen very angry and he hated it when his sister came over.

Grandma also had a dog named King. King was a large Shepherd-collie mix that was very lovable and playful. While King and Red got along very well, Stephen also felt that King dominated too much of Red's space.

After his father moved in, Stephen often sat staring at him intensely. He admired him. He would sit awake and listen to the going ons in his father's bedroom when his father brought a woman to the house for the night. Sometimes he would hear his father smacking them. This would often bring a smile to Stephen's face. He would imagine that each woman was his mother.

Ronald hadn't visited with his son much in the past, but now that he was living with him, he began to notice how his son was very demanding of Olivia.

"Get my food grandma," he would order her.

"You don't talk to your grandmother like that," his father warned him. Stephen just glared at his father as if he was crazy. Ignoring his father, he again demanded, "Grandma, where's my food."

"I said you don't talk to your grandmother like that. Apologize."

"No, she's just a woman," Stephen replied sharply.

Ronald was taken aback at his son's response at showing such ill regard for the woman who was taking care of him.

"Leave him alone Ronald," Olivia suggested protectively. She always protected Stephen.

"No, Stephen, go in your room until you can apologize to your grandmother."

Stephen went into the bedroom. It was a small closet sized bedroom. He sat across the twin bed, his back against the wall and began banging his head on the wall. He banged his head over and over and over until Grandma Olivia came in the room bringing him some food.

"There's something wrong with that kid," his father stated.

"Yes. There is," was all Olivia could respond. She felt Stephen had evil in him just like her Joseph.

Chapter Eleven

A sunny afternoon preceded Theresa's arrival at Grandma's for the summer. Theresa loved Grandma's dog King. He was very gentle with the kids, but Theresa was deathly afraid of Red, Olivia's big red alley cat. She didn't much like being around her brother either because he was always hitting her but she sure loved her grandmother.

Grandma always made her fried chicken wings or some fried mackerel. She always made her feel special. Stephen wanted Theresa to leave. She was invading his space. But Grandma made him play with her sometime. He sat outside staring at the dog. It was getting dark outside and they had just come back from throwing rocks at the bats that flew around the railroad tracks at dusk. As Theresa ran back towards the house, King instinctively started to follow her.

"No King, come with me," Stephen called to him.

Theresa continued to run towards the house and King turned around to follow Stephen.

"She's a girl," he said to King with annoyance, aggravated by the dog, "I'll teach you to listen to her so much."

Stephen walked along the edge of the tracks with King until they reached the opening that took them upon the tracks themselves. Stephen was not fearful of the freight or Amtrak trains that constantly roared by. They were just loud and sometimes shook the house. When an Amtrak train came by he and his sister would usually wave at the people until the entire train rolled by.

"Come on King! Let's go boy..." he called to him lovingly as King followed obediently.

As they reached the top step, Stephen looked to see if anyone was around. Sometime little white hoodlums hung out on the tracks but this time he was all alone on top of the railroad tracks. He took off the rope he had wrapped around his waist that he had stolen from Jackie's house. He grabbed King and proceeded to tie him to the railroad tracks. King just thought it was another game. He had tied him from his collar to both sides of the tracks.

A train should be coming any minute Stephen figured. He had sat on those railroad tracks enough to know what time the trains came by each day. He sat down on the edge of the tracks and waited as excitement welled up inside him when he saw the big light of the oncoming train and heard the continuous blowing whistle warning that the train would be arriving momentarily.

He sat on the high wall knowing he was dangerously close to the oncoming train and that if he wasn't careful the train could side swipe him off. As the train came swiftly barreling down, the conductor, mortified at seeing a dog tied to the tracks, knew it was too late to stop. He pulled down anxiously on the whistle hoping the dog would lie down and maybe the train would move over him.

The impact was quick. Stephen shifted swiftly hanging himself over the edge of the wall, leaving himself anchored just enough to watch as the train struck King crushing him and killing him instantly.

Stephen watched as the guts of the dog flew outwards. When the train had completely passed, Stephen smiled with satisfaction, jumped down from the high wall and ran back towards Grandma's house. As he approached the house, he heard his grandmother calling him and King.

She sounds worried he thought. The excitement of the possibility of being caught made him sweaty and the strong rush made him cry. He ran towards the house, face dirty with stained tears. He was breathing hard. When he got to the back door he shrieked loudly, "Grandma some white boys grabbed King and tied him to the railroad tracks and a train ran him over!" He started wailing and crying harder but inside he was pleased.

Olivia was grief stricken. She reached out to put her arms around Stephen but he just walked away. Theresa, who was sitting at the table eating her chicken wings, dropped the food that was in her hand and ran and hugged her grandmother as she cried. They held each other closely and moments later they heard Stephen banging his head against the wall. Bam! Bam! Bam!

But alas, all was not lost. Joannie Shield's dog had been impregnated by King and she gave Olivia one of its recent litters. Olivia named him Emperor, to follow in the footsteps of his dad. He looked just like his father, a small shepherd and collie mixed mutt. All he had to do was learn how to get along with the big mean alley cat and Stephen.

Chapter Twelve

14 Brinton Street - 1963

As soon as her divorce from Ronald Gonsalves was final, Rosetta married Donald Frye. It was a quick wedding because she was already pregnant with his first child. She gave birth to their son Ramon, August 10, 1960.

Don had been her prince charming. He moved them to what was thought to be a nice house at 14 Brinton Street located just off Washington Street in Roxbury. It was the last house on a dead end street.

At night, from the porch, they could see the Orange line commuter trains go by and hear the noise as well. It always sounded like they were right inside their house.

The orange and white trains traveled along tracks high off the ground on Washington Street. The track bases were in the middle of the street where cars and buses would have to drive in and out of or around them.

During the second year of their marriage, Don Frye had started coaching the Roxbury Boy's Club's swim team. He had gone to school to become a hair dresser but decided it wasn't lucrative enough to raise a family. He was a perfectionist and it took him too long to do one head. He continued to do hair on evenings and weekends. His vision was for a large family. Rosetta was again pregnant with her fifth child.

She gave birth to her youngest child on September 2, 1962. She named him Donald Ramon Frye, Jr. after her husband. She was tired. They were broke. She had no money for a new baby. She didn't want to breastfeed but it would help save money. This time her baby had to sleep in the dresser drawer. She didn't have a lot of help anymore and Donald wasn't a lot of help with neither the kids nor the housework.

After the baby, Donald decided the kids needed a dog. Just another thing to add to her chores, Rosetta felt, but it would make the kids happy. Don's old army buddy Gary Funches gave him a great big brown and black German shepherd named Baron.

Baron became their protector. Baron loved the kids. He was so big that Theresa and Ramon often rode on his back.

After Rosetta gave birth to their second child, Donald decided it was time for Rosetta to bring Stephen home.

Donald didn't understand why Rosetta didn't seem to have a liking for this child. He figured whatever the quandary had been, he was now the man of the house and could help him. Don felt Stephen needed a real man, a real father figure.

When the day came to pick Stephen up, Don and Rosetta, with Theresa tagging along, hailed a cab to go and get him. Don Frye's Oldsmobile was now inoperable, parked along the sidewalk in front of the house. He caught the bus to get to the Boys Club or he would walk.

When they arrived at 224 Lamartine Street, Olivia was standing in the doorway with Stephen, who stood somberly, his suitcase in hand.

He hadn't liked Donald Frye from the moment he had met him and his foolish mother had gone and married him. Everyone thought that Don Frye was the greatest guy in the world. "What a joke," Stephen scoffed to himself as the cab pulled up to the door.

Don Frye walked towards them greeting them kindly and thanking Olivia for all she does for the boy. Olivia felt since Don worked well with the kids at the Roxbury Boys Club, perhaps he may be able to bring Stephen out of his shell. Olivia took the suitcase from Stephen and handed it to Don who took it and put it in the trunk of the yellow cab.

"It's time for you to go back to your mama," Olivia instructed him warmly. She knew he didn't want to go. "His own father was too busy chasing women and never had time for Stephen. Perhaps a man could truly help him," Olivia hoped.

When Don went to take Stephen's hand, Stephen who was just six years old at this time, threw himself down onto the ground and began kicking and screaming.

Don Frye picked him up amidst the arm flailing and feet going in every direction and while enduring the continuous assault put Stephen in the back seat of the cab in between his mother and sister, then shut and locked the door. Don Frye got into the front seat. Rosetta tensed as her sons body leaned against hers. A small shudder shook through her.

The cab driver took off and headed for their home on 14 Brinton Street. Stephen sat banging his head against the cabs back seat and hummed quietly to himself. They neared Egleston Train Station and as soon as they turned and headed down Washington Street and were underneath the commuter railroad tracks Stephen swung open the back door to the cab and as he began falling out he grabbed the door and the car continued to move dragging Stephen along.

Theresa screamed. The cab driver slammed on the brakes. Stephen let go of the door, flew out of the cab, landing right beside it with his body sprawled spread eagle on his back in the middle of the street. At the same time a police car came careening around the corner. Its blazing siren was ear-piercing.

The police officer saw Stephen just as he hit the ground. He swiftly turned the steering wheel, stepping on his brakes just in time to avoid hitting the kid. He lost control of the squad car, slamming into a car from oncoming traffic. The police officer, unhurt, jumped out of the car and was able to check on everyone else. With all the commotion that happened in tandem, no one had been seriously hurt.

When the ambulance arrived, Stephen did not want to go to the hospital. He was bleeding from his head and Don Frye insisted the paramedics take him. After arriving at the hospital, they determined simply by looking that no x-rays were necessary and since he was coherent enough, they sent him home with ten stitches in the back of his head.

Chapter Thirteen

It didn't take long for Rosetta to grasp that life wasn't what she had expected it to be on 14 Brinton Street with Don Frye. She expected some tranquility but soon realized that her husband was a wife beater. It wasn't just the time he pushed her down when she was pregnant and didn't feel like walking to the store, it was a constant thing.

He would beat her up simply for having dinner late. His expectations were more than she could handle. She still worked at the sewing factory every day yet he didn't consider that much of a job even though it helped quite a bit towards their financial responsibilities.

Rosetta was afraid to come home most days. Sometimes she would send the kids to her mother-in-law, Consuelo Carter.

Known to the kids as Ma Carter, she along with her daughter Bunny and her son Snookie, lived just around the corner at 5 Codman Park on the first floor. The kids often ran over there when their mother was getting beat by Don.

No one ever did anything to stop him from beating her. They just kept the kids occupied and acted like Rosetta deserved it. Bunny would always do Theresa's hair which made Theresa cry every time because Bunny was very insensitive to her tender little head. Instead of sympathizing, she would take the comb and smack Theresa upside her head. Snookie never played uncle. He barely even said hello.

Sometimes Rosetta would run out of the house, run down the street and catch a cab to hide at her sister Tiny's house. She started smoking and drinking more and more. To avoid being beaten so regularly, she would meet Carole and her sister out at various night clubs. Being drunk took the pain away. At twenty-five she had five children and yet she looked as if she was forty-five years old. No longer did she favor the looks of Dorothy Dandridge, but instead, took on the appearance of an aged abused woman.

When Theresa was five, the neighbor in the connecting unit asked if Theresa could be the flower girl at her wedding and Don Frye said of course. Rosetta pressed and curled her daughter's hair styling it in a flip.

Theresa walked out of the door looking really cute in her white dress and basket of flowers. The bride's family drove Theresa to the wedding hall.

Walking down a church aisle is scary even for the bride. Theresa didn't know what a flower girl really was suppose to do and the panic she felt was indeed justified as she saw all the people marching into the church, taking their seats in the pews.

Just before the wedding began Theresa started crying. The makeup that had been put on her was dripping down onto her dress. The bride got really angry and snapped, "Have someone take her home!" She yelled hysterically, "I knew this wedding wouldn't go smoothly!"

The shrill of the bride's voice frightened Theresa even more but she was happy to be going home. When the man who drove her home dropped her off, when she opened the door and got out, he never even looked back to see if she made it onto the porch. He just left her on the sidewalk and rushed back to the wedding.

Theresa knocked on the door waiting for her mom or step-dad to open the door. When her step-dad finally appeared she ran into his arms, "I couldn't do it Donald! I couldn't do it," she cried, "I messed up Gina's wedding!"

"It's all right sweetheart," he said scooping her up into his arms, taking her inside. As Donald set her down, Theresa noticed that the house was strangely quiet and empty; even their dog Baron was gone.

"Where's mummy?" Theresa questioned.

"She moved out and left you and Stephen here with me!" he exclaimed.

"When is she coming back?" She was shaking, her voice worried.

"I don't really know," he told her as Stephen came from out of the bedroom to see who had come into the house.

"Well if you didn't hit mummy she wouldn't have left," Stephen stated malevolently. He looked at his sister, motioned for her to follow him as he turned and went back into their room. Theresa started to follow. Before she walked three steps away, Don told her, "Since your mother isn't here, you can take her place. After you change out of that dress you can get in there and start cleaning up the kitchen. You can take her place in the bedroom later too."

Theresa didn't exactly understand what he meant by that. Stephen who had his ear to the door certainly knew.

She was just five years old. She didn't know how to wash dishes. But because she was afraid of him, she would at least make an attempt. She dragged a chair from the kitchen table to stand on and started to wash the dishes.

The phone rang, startling her. She jumped down off of the chair and ran to get the telephone. It was mummy. "When are you coming home?" she asked her mother. Before Rosetta could answer, Don grabbed the telephone. "If you don't come home soon, your daughter will be taking your place in our bedroom," he said threateningly.

That wasn't giving Rosetta any other choice. She returned home. She would wait it out. Make a better plan to leave him later. "It won't be long," she thought. She couldn't let her daughter suffer like that as she wondered if he was really capable of molesting her little girl.

Rosetta, along with the kids, put up the façade of the happy family. Don Frye was a militant at the Boys' Club just like he was at home. Everyone felt it was due to his military background.

Anthony, who still admired Don Frye in spite of how he treated his mother, frequented the Boys' Club every day it was open which was every day except Sunday.

On Thursday, August 1, 1963, Anthony entered his sister in the Boys' Clubs of Boston 'Little Ms. Roxbury Contest' for the second time. Girls weren't really allowed at the Boys' Club except on Family Swim night.

Theresa would have to compete with almost one hundred contestants who vied for the spot. The first time she competed she was runner up. This time she won the title!

Theresa was crowned Little Miss Roxbury by Mayor John Collins' chunky daughter, Peggy. Anthony proudly stood by her side. She had her ribbon, she had her crown and they gave her a doll that was bigger than she was. Theresa hated it because it was white. She saw some of the other girls get small black baby dolls but because she was Little Miss Roxbury, she was given the biggest doll of them all which was suppose to be the best. She wanted to trade.

When she walked in the door at home she went to show it to Stephen. He snatched the doll out of her hands, tore its head off, threw it on the ground and stomped all over the face, smashing the plastic head to pieces. He walked away turned around, looked at his sister and smiled at her, "Congratulations!"

Chapter Fourteen

With the onset of Theresa starting kindergarten at the Higginson Elementary School, the neighborhood was in fear of a rapist that was plaguing the area. Rosetta told Stephen to make sure nothing happened to his sister on their way to school. Stephen wasn't fearful of the rapist bothering his sister. He had already had an encounter with the guy. It wasn't little girls he was looking for. It was little boys. He had taken Stephen into the bushes and pulled his pants down and played with his penis. Stephen had liked it.

Stephen never told anyone. He was simply annoyed each time his sister yelled, "Wait for me..." as they ran up the hill through the woods as they made their way through the shortcut to school. The only thing she had to worry about Stephen thought was the bulldog that chased them everyday.

He did feel sorry for his sister. He wasn't going to let anything happen to her as long as he could help it, and unless he did it himself. At five years old she was pretty much raising herself. He was standing outside the door when Ms. Heart, her kindergarten teacher, made her stand up as she walked over to Theresa, sniffed her and told her she was the one in the class who was making the room smell like piss. "You're a piss-pot," Miss Heart said meanly. Stephen watched as his sister put her head down shamefully against her chest.

Ms. Heart had four flat tires when she tried to head home that afternoon.

Chapter Fifteen

108 Talbot Ave - 1964

Don Frye thought it would be a good idea to move his family away from Roxbury, so in the summer of 1964, he moved them to 108 Talbot Ave, on the 2nd floor in Dorchester, MA. He thought it would be a safer neighborhood. But who were they to fear more than him they all wondered.

Rosetta continued to endure the constant beatings. Stephen seldom just stood by allowing it. He would always jump in. Once as Donald had his mother pinned to the ground, Stephen picked up a lamp and hit Donald upside the head with it knocking him out.

Soon all the kids began jumping into the constant fighting and ruckus. Whenever Donald hit their mother, one of them would blow a whistle and the others would come running. The neighbors from the floor below were always banging on the ceiling with a broom stick or something to get them to be quiet. Ironically the kids used the same broom technique on their own ceiling to quiet the family above them.

Don Frye was the best swimming instructor in the entire state of Massachusetts. No one would ever believe that Don Frye would ever hurt anyone even though he still had his militaristic ways. His public persona was a pretense but everyone bought into it. Everyone knew that he was a mean son of a bitch but they just figured he was tough on the swim team. That he wanted to breed winners.

Rosetta couldn't take the abuse any longer and after clever planning, one day as soon as Don left the apartment to head to the work, a moving truck pulled up to the door and Rosetta took her kids and moved into the Columbia Point Projects.

Chapter Sixteen

29 Montpelier Road - 1965

The Columbia Point Projects were built on top of a former garbage dump thrust on the edge of Boston Harbor. It was never an appealing place. Its yellow high rise buildings were desolate and institutional like in appearance. The one thousand five hundred and two units housed impoverished Blacks and a handful of White people. It was isolated geographically and culturally from Boston proper. Columbia Point was plagued by crime so severe that ambulances refused to go there. It was often referred to as the Cabrini-Greens of Boston.

But for the residents, it was home, feeling the isolation only when they tried to leave the "island". There was one way in and one way out. A sewage pumping station sat on the north side of the projects greatly resembling a castle. No one ever went near the castle. At night bats flew over the moonlit castle as if a scene from a Dracula movie. Most kids didn't realize that living in the projects was for the indigent.

Rosetta and her kids lived on the second floor of 29 Montpelier Road. It was a seven story building. There were several families with lots of kids so there were no limits to their imaginations for fun. The kids often played many games; Red Light, Green Light, Hide and go Seek, Giant Steps, Double Dutch.

There were two entrances into the building. Most days they sat on the back steps of 29 Montpelier Road where they all ended up with their friends. Theresa's best friend Barbara lived underneath them with her brother Ken and her two sisters Viola and Ann. Barbara and Theresa were the same age and their brothers Ken and Ramon were the same age.

Often times they would make forts or clubhouses out of cardboard boxes they took from the dumpster at the Stop & Shop Market down the street or they would use old mattresses that someone threw out for the garbage man.

They built their clubhouses in the hallway or on the side of the building under the second floor roofing. Sometimes they would go into these hiding places and would explore sexuality by dry humping or grinding. Theresa would be with Ken and Barbara would be doing it with either Ramon or Donald. These humping sessions never lasted long. They always heard people in the hallway and were really afraid of what they were doing. Although afraid they did enjoy what they were feeling. They were too young to understand.

Theresa shared a bedroom with her brothers Donald, Stephen and Ramon. At night her brothers Stephen, Ramon and Donald would take turns pulling down her panties and their underwear and grind on her. She was in the second grade, but strangely enough her young body enjoyed it and she didn't complain. Sometimes they hurt her when they were grinding their penis on her pelvic bone.

Nights were not welcome very much in their house though. Before Stephen would go to sleep he would bang his head on the wall for at least an hour and hum. "Mom…can you make him stop," they would yell ... But he wouldn't stop. This was a constant occurrence. When he finally did go to sleep his sister Theresa, afraid to go to the bathroom in the dark, would go and pee on him so she wouldn't get in trouble for wetting the bed. The bathroom was right next to their bedroom, but she was afraid of all the roaches that scattered the floors at night.

Chapter Seventeen

It was a late Sunday fall afternoon when Stephen spotted Lauren alone in the hallway. She was the average size for a four year old. Her white skin was pale as a white magnolia. She had brown baby fine hair that was cut short below her ears almost in a boyish fashion, with bangs cut straight across the middle of her forehead. She wore a white laced short sleeved eyelet blouse that buttoned down the front, green cotton shorts, white anklet socks and white sneakers outlined with pink.

Lauren's family had just moved to the fourth floor of 29 Montpelier Road three weeks earlier. There were only three other white families living in the entire Columbia Point projects and two of them lived at 29 Montpelier Road.

It was very quiet in the hallway and there were no sounds of other kids coming from outside. Lauren had never seen Stephen in the building before. He wondered how she got out of the apartment by herself. The doors on the apartments were very heavy. He looked at her and smiled.

He still had some candy in his pocket from when Doc's candy truck came around. Whenever the white truck came all the kids would run to it with their pennies to buy candy. Anthony worked on the truck and often Stephen would get his candy for free. He went in his pockets and took the candy out to show Lauren. He held it out in front of her.

"Hi, I have some candy. What's your name?"

"Lauren," she said coyly with a smile as only a four year old innocent girl could smile.

"Hey, if you come with me, I will give you some lollipops," Stephen told her holding out his hand showing her the candy again.

Lauren did not hesitate to take his hand.

He walked her up five flights of stairs to the seventh floor roof. The door to the roof was always unlocked. After walking her to a remote area of the roof, where no one in any other building could see them, he continued his seduction of Lauren. A light breeze blew in the air.

"Lauren, take off your clothes," he told her in a soft yet manly voice making himself sound older than he really was, "and I will give you this red lollipop!"

"Okay," she responded. Still smiling she unbuttoned her blouse and quickly pulled her arms out of the openings of the eyelet blouse. Then she pulled off her pants and held her hand out for the lollipop.

"No, Lauren, you didn't take your socks and underwear off."

Lauren smiled at him again. Stephen took that as teasing.

"Okay."

She took off her panties that had the word 'Sunday' scripted on them. Most four year olds and even older girls wore panties with the days of the weeks on them and Lauren was proud of hers. She took off her socks and stood completely naked in front of him. She held out her hand again. He laughed sardonically, but spoke playfully to her.

"Okay, here's the red one! Now how about if you give me a hug for the purple one!"

Lauren ran into his arms without fear. He held her there for a minute, but it seemed longer to him. He rubbed his hands down her back to her buttocks. "She's so soft" he thought to himself. He was mesmerized. Then he let her go.

"Do you want me to take my clothes off too?" he asked her. She looked at him strangely, scrunching up her nose as if to say "what?!" and before she could answer he had pulled down his pants.

"Hey! What does this look like to you?" he asked Lauren as he held his small boyish penis in his hand for her to see. "Does it look like a popsicle?"

"Yes," she said giggling, "My brother has a wee-wee too." He held a lollipop in his hand and pulled the wrapper off. "Look Lauren. You suck a wee-wee just like you suck this lollipop." He demonstrated to her and had her try it with her lollipop.

Suddenly a fear set in him. "Someone must be looking for her by now," he thought, "Why am I doing this to this little girl. I better take her back down stairs."

His young mind was not thinking straight. He had picked up her socks but forgot that she was naked. As they quietly proceeded down the first flight of stairs, Lauren began asking for her clothes. When her voice started to rise, Stephen stuffed one of the socks in her mouth and rushed her down to the bottom floor. He was relieved no one had seen them.

Theresa and Barbara were sitting outside on the back entrance steps when they saw the little four year old white girl walk out of the building. She stood in front of them completely naked with a lollipop in her hand, a sock in her mouth, her brown hair tousled all over her head.

Stephen had crept quietly behind the girl disappearing from her sight after walking her down from the roof using the back stairway where the incinerator was always afire. He hid behind the raggedy iron door that was partially open. He wanted to watch the reactions of others when they saw her. He stood back in the doorway out of sight. As he watched, all he could think about was how soft and cuddly she felt. His small juvenile penis was erect again at the thought.

"Oh my God!" Theresa exclaimed, her hand going to cover her mouth, when she spotted Lauren walking toward her and Barbara. Lauren was completely naked. "What happened Lauren?" she asked taking the sock out of the little girl's mouth. "Where are your clothes?"

"I got a lollipop from a man," she replied solemnly yet with a slight smile. It wasn't cold but her nakedness now made her shiver.

"Barbara run upstairs and get her mom!" Theresa ordered as she looked around to see if she could find something to cover the little girl. As she looked, she saw the other neighboring kids turn the corner heading towards the building. Before the kids got to the building Theresa glanced up into the entry way and saw the back stairway door closing slowly. She swore she saw her brother Stephen, sneaking swiftly up the stairs.

The other kids stared at Lauren's nakedness.

"Where are your clothes at?" one asked.

"A man gave me a lollipop if I took them off," she replied matter of factly.

"Did he do something to you?" another child asked with unknowing insensitivity. These kids were older and had heard plenty of things about sex.

"Did he stick his thing inside you?"

"What did he look like?"

The thoughtlessness of the children startled Lauren. Lauren wasn't sure what she had done wrong but she could hear in their voices that something just wasn't right. Unsure of herself she put the lollipop in her mouth to show them. She started to suck the lollipop seductively and afterwards told them, "This is how the man showed me he wanted me to do to his wee-wee."

Her mother appeared frantically with a blanket, just in time to hear her daughter's comment. She grabbed her daughter, wrapped the blanket around her and ran quickly back up the stairs to their apartment. This was no longer home to their family. That evening they moved out as quickly as they had moved in and were never seen again in the projects.

All the other kids of 29 Montpelier Road were on the look out for a man they didn't know. He became a fearful unknown person. For a long time all the children ran in and out of their apartments as quickly as possible. They could hardly have imagined the *man* was among them.

Weeds began to grow in the stomach of Stephen's first silent victim.

Chapter Eighteen

Ronnie Chambers came to live with the family while they were at 29 Montpelier Road. He was one of Ronald Gonsalves' illegitimate kids, son of Juanita.

Because he got along with Rosetta better than his own mom he wanted to move in with them. He wanted to know his brothers and sisters. Surprisingly Rosetta didn't object although he was a constant reminder of her ex-husband and his infidelities.

Ronnie and Stephen instantly bonded and began hanging out together; often vying to show their muscles off and see who was the strongest. Their brother Anthony had formed an alliance with his friend Lawrence who lived above them on the third floor at 29 Montpelier Road.

Though not enemies they often played tricks on one another. The four of them had walked down the street to the Stop and Shop the only grocery store in the vicinity of the projects at the time. It was a common place for thefts. While none of them were starving, it was just something to do to steal food from the local grocers. So this was another typical visit for them. They separated as they got into the store each in groups of two and began stuffing steaks down into their shirts. As Ronnie and Stephen walked out ahead of them, they stopped to talk to the security guard,

"Hey there are two boys back there stealing steaks they stuffed down their shirts," Stephen informed him.

"One is really tall," Ronnie Chambers explained to the guard.

"And the other has a big mole on the side of his nose," Stephen revealed as he described his brother Anthony.

With that done, they walked out the door.

"We probably shouldn't have done that!" Ronnie said feeling a bit guilty, "Let's go."

"No. I want to watch them get arrested," Stephen said with absolutely no remorse.

As Lawrence and Anthony walked through the exit doors of the Stop and Shop, the security guard followed.

"Hey!" he called out to them his gun aimed, "Hold it right there!"

They stopped and waited for the guard to approach.

"What do you have in your shirts?"

They had no choice but to take the steaks out that they were planning on having for dinner that evening!

"Damn man," Ronnie said, "Moms is going to be mad at us!" They watched them get handcuffed.

"Yeah," laughed Stephen wickedly. "Let's go cook our steak."

Chapter Nineteen

Fight Day at 29 Montpelier Road

Roy Jones was Rosetta's current boyfriend when they lived at 29 Montpelier Road. She had had more than a few, but he stayed around the longest even though he hated the children as much as they couldn't stand him. He was a fat ass light-skinned black man who always wanted to eat. Rosetta spent plenty of time serving him. The kids always felt he was taking food off their table and wasn't providing any.

It was a Sunday morning and the sound of his yelling and beating on Rosetta had awakened all the kids.

Theresa banged on the door yelling for her mom. "Get the hell away from the door," Roy hollered back at her. Anthony figured it was his mother's business as he took his sister and made her go back to her room.

Ronnie Chambers and Stephen were not going to tolerate what was going on. They ran to the phone dialed zero for the operator and told her it was an emergency;

please send the police. It was the projects so who knew how long it would take before they would arrive.

The bedroom had quieted and both Stephen and Ronnie's imagination ran wild as they envisioned Roy killing their mother. Stephen picked up a big thick chain they had stolen off of a fence a while ago and ran and kicked his mother's door open yelling, "Leave my mother alone or I will kill you."

Roy jumped up off the bed about to assault him when Ronnie appeared showing that he was ready to take him on as well. "Everything's okay," Rosetta yelled back to the kids sticking her head out from under the covers so they could see her face and just as she did, they heard yelling coming from the apartment just below them. The boys ran to the kitchen window.

Alvin Steele was trying to get into his apartment and the door had sweated so much that it wouldn't open and he couldn't get in. However, Alvin thought his girlfriend Gloria Williams was trying to lock him out.

"Look bitch if you don't open the door I am going to kick it in," Alvin threatened knowing it was just a small threat as the doors were way too heavy for anyone to be able to kick in.

"Alvin, I can't get the door open. It's stuck," Gloria shouted back to him, trying to explain that it wasn't her fault.

She was leaning out the kitchen window talking to him. But Alvin was drunk, a constant state of his. He wasn't hearing it. Suddenly and unexpectedly, Alvin jumped over the four foot spiked fence that had been just been put up around the buildings, jumped up into the living room and as he jumped into the living room window, Gloria, frightened and not wanting another ass whooping, jumped out of the kitchen window. She didn't have any shoes on and was in her night gown. She climbed over the spiked fence which caught her gown, ripping it slightly. Once cleared from the fence, she took off running as fast as she could. Alvin ran from the living room to the kitchen, stuck his head out the window, saw Gloria turn the corner, then he jumped back out through the kitchen window and over the spiked fence and began chasing her.

In the meantime, Stephen was watching out the window at what was going on. He grabbed a baseball bat, quickly ran down the one flight of stairs and went after Alvin. As Gloria, Alvin, and then Stephen rounded the corner, the police finally showed up and as they got out of the car, a woman from the next building over, that was connected to 29 Montpelier Road, stuck her head out of her fourth floor apartment window and yelled, *"Help Police this man...."* and before she could finish her sentence, she jumped out of the window and landed flat on her back, just missing the spiked fence!

As the police eyed the situation, they had to swiftly decide which case of domestic violence to respond to first. They called for back up and an ambulance.

When the ambulance arrived, Gloria came limping and bleeding around the corner with Stephen as he held the bat in his hand to protect her. Alvin stayed back hiding in another building because there were warrants out for his arrest. He hadn't been able to catch Gloria because he was caught off guard when he saw the kid upstairs coming after him with a baseball bat!

A paramedic went to Gloria when they saw all the bleeding. She was bleeding from all the glass she had stepped on while running from Alvin. She refused treatment and just headed back into the house still being escorted by Stephen.

Additional paramedics loaded the woman who had jumped out the window into the ambulance. She had landed directly on her back. Her vital signs were normal but she was unconscious. She suffered miraculously from one broken index finger.

Once the ambulance departed, the police went back to the door to respond to their original call. Roy and Rosetta were now snuggled in the bed. Rosetta went to the door and said, "It must have been a mistake."

After the police left, Roy glared at Ronnie and Stephen, "Don't ever call the police on me again." Stephen responded with a look that even scared a big man like Roy. "Don't put your hands on my mother again."

Roy was run from the house afterwards. The kids had had enough of their mother being physically abused by men in her life. "If you can't keep your kids in place, then I am out of here." Rosetta felt it was perhaps a good idea. Her boys were getting older and no longer tolerant of any man hitting her. She feared what she felt they were capable of doing to another man who put their hands on her.

Her oldest son was in a small neighborhood gang and was often referred to as Gunsy. Stephen was strong and could easily kill. She could think it. She could visualize her older boys going in the wrong direction. She had heard the gang refer to her daughter as Lil Gunsy. She couldn't bear to live it. So not only was it time for Roy to go. It was time to get her kids out of the projects. And then the shot rang out.

Chapter Twenty

Martin Luther King

April 5, 1968 - The Friday morning headlines were the same all over the United States: Martin Luther King, Jr. had been assassinated.

"At 6:01 p.m. on April 4, 1968, a shot rang out. Dr. Martin Luther King, Jr., who had been standing on the balcony of his room at the Lorraine Motel in Memphis, TN, now lay sprawled on the balcony's floor. A gaping wound covered a large portion of his jaw and neck. A great man who had spent thirteen years of his life dedicating himself to nonviolence had been fallen by a sniper's bullet."

The morning was cloudy with small scattered showers. But the weatherman had said it would all clear up by the afternoon.

President Johnson had summoned the Negro leaders. The death of Martin Luther King had triggered violence.

The violence in Boston was mostly directed in the Dudley Street area. But what was happening wasn't

Martin's dream. The streets weren't filled with non-violence, just the opposite. There were angry Blacks tipping over police cars, attacking whites but mostly setting fires and destroying their *own* neighborhoods. Dudley Street would never be the same again.

Rosetta, with her children, stayed in the apartment. Columbia Point had been blocked off by the police. It was as if they had been imprisoned themselves. W.I.L.D, the most popular Black radio station in the city, kept them abreast as to what was going on in the outskirts of the projects as they consistently pleaded to the community to respect Martin's dreams and let his legacy move us, instead of his assassination. Phone calls into the project let them know how other family members were fairing.

Rosetta just sat there with a cigarette in her hand paralyzed. She was afraid, afraid for her entire race.

Ronnie, Anthony and Stephen managed to sneak out of Columbia Point and meet up with their cousin Claudia to go to a community meeting that was being held by various ministers of the community at the Roxbury Boys Club. The boys really just wanted to see what was going on outside of the projects.

What they saw was more than their youthful years could fathom. The city in complete turmoil. Unfortunately, time has yet to heal this deep wound.

Chapter Twenty-One

15 Greendale Road

It was January of 1969, when they moved out of the projects and into the brown wooden three story house at 15 Greendale Road in Mattapan. Rosetta's kids were 7, 9, 11, 13 and 15. So young, yet they seemed so much older. Mattapan seemed so far away from the projects. It was like a whole new world for them and they were starting a new life. They felt free, as if just released from a prison island that isolated them from the outside world.

Ronnie Chambers had gone back to live with his own family. Though he loved his brother and enjoyed their camaraderie this made Stephen very happy. Theresa had developed a crush on him, as did every woman Ronnie came in contact with. Ronnie use to always tell her, "If you weren't my sister, I would marry you." She would simply blush and smile at him. Stephen hated the way she would look at their brother and blush. But he hated even more that Theresa didn't like any women around her brother Ronnie! She had a huge crush on him.

Rosetta had taken the house at 15 Greendale Road, just to get the kids out of the project. She couldn't really afford the rent. It was a four bedroom house and it would be the first time Theresa would have her own room. Anthony being the oldest had his own room and the other three shared one bedroom. When Stephen didn't like the idea, he started staying at his Grandma's again on the weekends and during the summer.

It had been the middle of the school year, but Rosetta wanted out of the projects as quickly as possible. By this time, Anthony was in the tenth grade at Boston English High School. Stephen was in the seventh grade and had just started attending Solomon Lewenberg Junior High. Theresa was in the sixth grade, Ramon was in the 4th grade and Donald was in the 2nd grade. The youngest three attended the same school, the Audubon Elementary School.

Regrettably while the move was good for their well being, it was the beginning of the children separating from each other. While neither of Rosetta's ex-husbands paid child support, Rosetta had to financially provide for her children on her own.

She somehow found a way to cheat the welfare system and continue working. She realized she was spending too much money on rent and decided after six months and with school out for the summer, they had to move from 15 Greendale Road.

Chapter Twenty-Two

71 Goodale Road

71 Goodale Road was a three family house in which Rosetta moved her family into the second floor. It was just two streets away from Greendale Road, up the hill off Wellington Hill Street.

They had a separate entrance to their apartment but had to run down a flight of stairs to let people in. It was a smaller place with a more affordable rent. The home had two bedrooms, a dining room and the living room with a huge hallway.

Rosetta decided her four sons could share a room and Theresa would have the dining room that was located in the middle of the house, open for anyone who walked by to see. Though a crowded house, Anthony decided to get a dog for the family. He named her Wendy. Wendy was a shiny black mutt. She was very smart and very well housebroken. When in heat, she was often getting stuck with the dog named Bandit, who lived around the corner.

Bandit belonged to Roderick Williams who was a friend of the family who lived around the corner.

The Williams family had a small record shop located on Blue Hill Ave. Roderick and his brother, Reggie, were always at the record shop. They were both handsome young men. Roderick was rather short with a small afro and small in stature. Theresa use to visit the record shop often because she had a crush on Roderick.

It was also home to where she would often buy her Jackson Five albums and posters. The smell of incense often saturated the place. Theresa use to think of it as the *'Psychedelic Shack'* when she visualized the words to the Temptations' hit of that name.

Wendy and Bandit had a couple of litters together. Wendy decided she would have her babies on Theresa's bed. When they let Wendy out to go to the bathroom they would move the puppies to a blanket on the floor, but when Theresa went to school the puppies would be back on her bed by the time she came home.

Wendy and Theresa both were devastated when three of the puppies were found dead. It looked as if their necks had been broken. It happened the day Stephen came home from Grandmother's.

By the age of sixteen Stephen barely went to school, barely bathed and slept on the couch all day long until he had to get up to go to work. On the nights when he didn't go to work, he would simply watch Johnny Carson. The boy loved Johnny Carson and Elvis Presley.

The funk of his under arms permeated throughout the entire living room. The other kids in the house couldn't even sit in the living room to watch television when he was around. When anyone else in the family wanted to watch television they were confronted with the wrath of Stephen. He would lie with blankets that weren't washed for over a year that carried his stench, completely covering himself from head to toe. If anyone disturbed him they would get a shoe thrown at them or whatever was within his reach, a vase, a book, a spoon, even a knife.

All of his siblings were afraid of him because he had somehow found a love for karate and become a karate expert. The younger two weren't affected so much by him because after school and every Saturday, Donald and Ramon would normally go to the Roxbury Boys club as they were part of the swimming and diving team. No, actually, they *were* the swimming and diving team. Their father, Don Frye, was still the coach and he made sure they were the best in New England.

While the move from Columbia Point had put a dent in the kids' closeness, Theresa, Ramon and Donald, whenever the three were at home, would have happy times. They would often stand in Theresa's room loudly singing Jackson Five songs. They all loved the Jackson Five and Theresa had all of their albums. She also had two hundred and ten pictures of them on her wall. Sometimes the kids singing drove their mother crazy, especially when they all tried to sing the song, Who's Lovin' You.

She had noticed they were each going off in different directions, but it also made her smile when they sang together. It was amazing how the music of the Jackson Five held her youngest kids together.

Chapter Twenty-Three

4A Forest Street – Grandma's house

In 1969, Grandma Olivia had moved as well. She moved from the house that the kids had loved at 224 Lamartine Street in Jamaica Plain. The owner had put it up for sale. When she went to pick up her old alley cat Red, to put in the car, to take to her new place, he tried to bite her. Olivia threw him down and left him there.

She moved to a three bedroom apartment at 4A Forest Street in Roxbury, MA. One extra bedroom was for Theresa and if Stephen came over Olivia would have Theresa use her room. Grandma for some reason only had a small twin sized bed to sleep in. She had also taken in a border to help her with the rent. His name was Sidney Vaughan. He was a very lanky tall man almost reaching the top of the doorway. He had a long horse shaped face with very smooth dusty russet brown skin, thin eyes and a long nose. He looked to be about in his late sixties.

Theresa went over to Grandma's house every weekend where the rituals continued. Friday nights,

Grandma would fry mackerel for Theresa and she still made fried chicken wings for both Theresa and Stephen. Stephen was always there and Theresa still hated that, but no one could keep her away from her grandmother, not even her crazy ass brother. He would do the same thing over at their grandmother's. Sleep all day long and do nothing. Sometimes he would yell at Olivia but she wasn't afraid of him. She was the only one who could see through him. She loved him for being her grandson, but was saddened at the monster she felt dwelled within his soul.

Sidney was very seldom seen in the house. He was simply the border Grandma had taken in. He had the biggest room in the house. It was enormous.

On Saturday mornings, Sidney would sometimes sit in the kitchen with Theresa as she had her toast and tea. Grandma served her tea with milk in little English tea cups and saucers that were white with small red roses embedded on them.

Every now and then Sidney would come in the living room to sit with Olivia to watch a Red Sox game. Olivia was an avid Red Sox fan often cheering for the likes of Carl Yastrzemski and Tony Conigliaro.

Other than those infrequent rare moments, you only knew Sidney was home when you heard his slippered feet shuffling to and from the bathroom.

Three days had gone by when grandma realized she hadn't seen nor heard Sidney come out of his room. She stood outside his door calling his name. After not getting a response, she sent Stephen in the room to check on him.

Stephen had smelled death the moment he entered the room. He surveyed the room as he walked in. The large dingy room was dark as Sidney had always kept it. The thick curtains that hung in the window were closed. On his night stand next to his bed, Sidney kept a picture of an unknown woman. "Was that his mother?" Stephen wondered as he stared at the picture. She was beautiful. He picked up the picture and kissed it.

The colors or design of the bedspread on his king size bed were barely recognizable. Sidney was lying in his bed, face up on his back … dead.

Stephen sat on the edge of the bed and looked closely at the body and pushed it. He was curious about old rotting death. Roaches had swarmed the bed, crawling in and out of Sidney's eyes. Maggots were eating at his flesh.

Theresa wasn't at Grandma's when they discovered the body. But she was there the weekend they determined Sydney had died and in the middle of the night she had seen Stephen closing Sidney's door as she drowsily came out of the bathroom.

It took the coroners' office over five hours to send someone for the body. There was no autopsy. He was an old man with no family and they simply concluded he died of loneliness.

After they removed his body, Stephen immediately packed up Sidney's stuff, threw it outside for the garbage man and moved into the room. He kept the framed picture of the woman that was on the night stand next to Sidney's bed.

Chapter Twenty-Four

Spring 1972

Joseph Gonsalves was released from prison in early 1972 with explicit instructions to stay away from little girls younger than eighteen years old. This complicated his relationship with his mother. She refused to stop having her granddaughter Theresa over and by doing so was refusing to see him. She had not visited him one time while he was in prison, but she did send food, she wrote him letters and she sent him money.

He retreated to Worcester, MA where he decided to start life over. He was a grown man now and his experience in prison took away any desire to go back.

He got a job as a laborer for a construction company. He dated many women and then he met Mary Costa. She was also from the Cape Verdean Islands. While Mary became the love of his life, it was a clouded relationship. They both were hard alcoholics and he often beat her up, apologizing over and over only when sober.

The police no longer responded to calls from their residence.

Mary just didn't know what to do to make Joseph happy, until he finally told her what it would take.

"I want your daughter," he told Mary. "I want Marie."

There was no hesitation; there was no stuttering on his part. He pointedly told her what he wanted; what he needed. It would take her giving him her daughter to make their relationship work, to keep him from other little girls.

Her daughter of the same name, whom they called Marie to separate themselves to others, was the spitting image of her mother as a young girl. She was fifteen years old, with big wide brown eyes, a warmish brown creamy skin tone, short brown curly hair, and a look of total innocence that attracted men like a flower attracts a bee. Her shape, however, was still that of a child with budding small breast.

Joseph proceeded to tell Mary as much as he cared to disclose about his past. Told her the urges still haunted him, this craving, this lust he had for young girls. He never told her or anyone about Cherene, the last little girl he had raped, but the first little girl he strangled to death before leaving Sao Vicente. He often reminisced about that day. It still seemed like yesterday to him and he could still smell the sweet scent of her youthful body.

He had told Mary that he wanted Marie; that she was what he needed to make him happy. Sadly, Marie was all too willing to oblige. She had found him attractive and yet she was fearful of him, this older strong man. She went to his bed willingly. This turned them into a happy family. While they were still drunkards, the fighting stopped. Mary and Marie took turns sleeping with Joseph.

Marie had just turned sixteen when she found herself pregnant with Joseph's child. She was overjoyed. But he was nervous as hell. Out of fear of going back to prison for rape, he married her.

Mary was heartbroken but there was nothing she could do. She had condoned the relationship. It had kept him from menacing other young girls. Marie gave birth to Richard. And even after giving birth she was still young enough to appease Joseph's urges for the younger flesh.

Chapter Twenty-Five

Olivia felt Stephen would be better off if he wasn't in the house so much, maybe get a damn job instead of sleeping all day. At her request, Jackie Shields who had been her neighbor at 224 Lamartine Street, was able to get Stephen a job at the Fantasia Restaurant in Cambridge, MA working in the kitchen.

Surprisingly, he was a diligent worker and when there was a need for additional help, he in turn recommended his friend Roderick for the job.

Stephen and Roderick seemed to always be competitive with one another. They were both practicing Karate students working with the same Sensei.

Roderick, although aware of Theresa's crush on him, wasn't aware that Stephen's hidden agenda was to keep him away from his sister. When Stephen stayed at his mothers, Roderick would drive around the corner in his 1972 black Dodge Charger to pick Stephen up for work, but if Stephen wasn't ready, Roderick would just leave him. Stephen would simply hop on his bike and peddle his way from Mattapan to Cambridge, an almost ten mile bike ride. Roderick figured it must have been part of the energy derived from Stephen's karate stamina.

Stephen and Roderick had developed their friendship in Junior high. They were both eighth graders at the Solomon Lewenberg Junior High School. The school was located at the top of Wellington Hill and just a few short blocks from the Boston State Mental Hospital in Mattapan.

They were in the same classroom and Stephen was trying to look over Roderick's shoulder to copy off of his paper and when Roderick caught him, Stephen jumped out of his chair, grabbed Roderick's paper, tore it into little pieces and threw in on the floor.

It was a strange combination, the two of them, yet they seemed to bring out the competitive edge in one another. Roderick was one of two kids in the entire school who wasn't afraid of Stephen. There was only one time when Roderick did fear him when for absolutely no reason at all Stephen snatched Roderick's sweater from him and continuously stabbed it over and over. He showed no emotion about it and handed Roderick the sweater back in shreds. Roderick had seen at least three different sides of Stephen. He wrote it off to moodiness.

However, Stephen's reputation preceded him. Pierson was the other boy who wasn't afraid of him. Pierson was a wrestler who always felt that wrestlers were better than the so called karate experts. He felt he could easily beat this kid who walked around the school intimidating everyone. So he decided to call Stephen out to fight. But what was supposed to be a fight turned into instant misery for Pierson. Stephen merely made one quick karate move and knocked Pierson out. Immediately, Roderick wanted to know who his Karate teacher was and if Stephen would teach him his techniques. Pierson changed his tune and also decided to switch to karate.

After word got out around the Solomon Lewenberg Junior High School, Stephen was left alone. While they all called him crazy, they would pay him money to see how many push ups he could do during gym or anytime after school.

Stephen and Roderick shared many secrets together and on the days when Stephen did go to school, they normally hung out at lunch until the history teacher began taking Stephen off school grounds.

Roderick thought it strange that a teacher would take Stephen to lunch, particularly with his horrible grades…but then just figured it was a way Stephen was scamming for free food and a way to get out of class.

Mr. Higgins, their history teacher, was very frumpy and hippie-like. Often unshaven, he sported a disheveled mustache and long hair. Stephen and Mr. Higgins would leave the school grounds every Tuesday at 11:00. Mr. Higgins lived close by the school. He would pick up some McDonald's and take Stephen to his house. Mr. Higgins interest was in more than just feeding the kid. He knew the kid was quiet. Felt the kid was odd, yet dangerous. But to put Stephen at ease, he began treating him like a son. He bought him gifts, they played card games. Stephen was a very willing pupil.

Stephen, however, wasn't being fooled as Mr. Higgins thought. He knew the seduction act as he had played it out in his mind so many times. He had often dreamed of doing this to other little boys, but first he wanted it done to himself.

After his experiment with Mr. Higgins, Stephen terminated the relationship. His continuing school years were filled with suspensions, bad grades and his always being in some sort of trouble.

So after starting high school, when he got expelled the first time from Dorchester High, he decided it was unnecessary to go back and dropped out of school completely.

When he wasn't practicing karate, his days went back to consisting of sleeping on the couch until it was time for him to go to work.

Chapter Twenty-Six

There was a seemingly soft side to Stephen as well. He would give his coat to a kid who stood freezing in the snow and would in turn freeze himself, yet, he didn't want to help the old guy getting beat up and robbed.

And there was the time he rode his bike home in the rain from Fantasia with a cake in one hand to make sure his little brother Donald had a cake for his tenth birthday.

Because he was very over protective of Roderick, there was no room for Roderick to allow any other friends in his life at the time. Stephen was always around consuming his time. And with Roderick's obsession with karate, he chose to hang around Stephen with hopes of learning some of his techniques. He admired that about him.

In the beginning of the summer, Roderick's bike was stolen. It was a high quality bike with the best gimmicks. Roderick saw the kid taking off on his bike but there was nothing he could do about it. Two weeks later,

Stephen and Roderick were at the movie theatre. A new Bruce Lee film was playing... 'Enter the Dragon'!

After getting their popcorn, as they walked down the theater aisle, Roderick noticed a familiar boy they passed by him.

"Hey Stephen...there's that kid that stole my bike!" Roderick whispered in surprise.

"Are you sure?"

"Yeah that's him alright, Lamont."

Stephen reached in his pocket and pulled out a surprise, a 22 caliber pistol. Fear immobilized Roderick for a fleeting moment. "Where the hell did you get that thing from?"

"Don't worry about it. I'm just going to go and kill him for taking your bike," Stephen told him matter-of-factly.

"No. Are you crazy?" Roderick panicked, "It was just a bike, let it go."

"Naw, he can't just take your bike and get away with it. Let's go," Stephen said walking back to where Lamont was sitting.

"No man, don't do anything. Just let it go," Roderick panicked.

Stephen wasn't listening. He walked up to Lamont and pointed the gun down into his face.

"Whoa, Whoa, Whoa...what's this about?" Lamont asked as putting his hands up as if Stephen was a cop. He certainly knew who Stephen was and had heard about how crazy he was said to be.

"You stole my friend's bike," It wasn't a question, it was stated as fact.

"No man," Lamont started to exclaim.

"Shut up! Don't' lie. Start running as fast as you can. If I can still see you when I finish counting to three, I'll just kill you. And make sure Roderick's bike gets back to him."

Lamont jumped up out of his seat and took off running as fast as he could.

Stephen laughed the sinister indescribable laugh he had, as he counted out loud to three. Patrons in the theater yelled to him to shut up. There were no bullets in the gun. He had stolen it from his history teacher's house and just kept it in his pocket.

Roderick's bike appeared on his lawn before he arrived home.

Chapter Twenty-Seven

Theresa still annoyed the hell out of Stephen. He was sick of her little crush on Roderick. She was always stopping in the record shop Roderick's family owned. Yet through all her annoyance, Stephen couldn't help noticing how sexy she was becoming. She had some big legs on her. She walked a lot and ran track. She wore mini skirts with sweatshirts and sneakers.

Tomorrow, November 24, 1973 would be her fifteenth birthday, "Tomorrow you will be fifteen years old...ripe and ready for me," Stephen whispered to her as he passed her by. She heard him loudly and clearly as she rolled her eyes at him.

"Oh well," Stephen thought, "She may not like it but this is a crazy world and without me here to protect her, she would get touched by someone else. I don't want another person to be the first she gets touched by. It's my right as her brother that I am her first."

His thoughts continued as he lied under the covers on the couch. "She thinks it should be Michael Jackson. He ain't thinking about her! That's all she thinks about is Michael Jackson, Michael Jackson. Well I am better than he is and she has another thing coming."

Yes, Theresa had heard every word he said to her. "Crazy bastard," she said loud enough for him to hear. From that day on, Theresa became guarded and truly fearful of her own brother. She began having restless nights as he slept on the couch in the living room. Her room was the open dining room area, so she had no doors. A room divider covered with her younger brothers' eighty-eight swimming and diving trophies blocked any view into her room from the living room but all other areas were open. She had no privacy. If she came home from school and he was there alone she would leave as quickly as possible and go to a friend's house until her mother came home. He never did anything around the house. After starting his Karate stuff, he decided that only women needed to do housework and should be subservient, having food on the table for him every night. He was always saying to Theresa and his mother, "Women in Japan do all the work. You need to be more like Japanese women."

Shortly after Xmas, thankfully for Theresa, their mother announced she had just bought a new house in Mattapan and Theresa would have her own room. She didn't have an open line of communication with her mother so she didn't bother telling her what her brother had said to her. Hell she had her first period at eleven and now here she was fifteen and her mother still didn't know.

Rosetta didn't know the tremendous amount of relief that her daughter just breathed after learning she would have her own room.

It was the end of 1973.

Chapter Twenty-Eight

21 Cookson Terrace (1974)

Rosetta had worked hard to purchase her first piece of property. Here she was a double divorcee and single mother with five kids who didn't receive any child support from her kids fathers. She was proud of her accomplishment.

She was good at whatever job she worked at and she loved her job at the Roxbury Comprehensive Community Health Center.

The house was a nice size house for the family. It had an attic that became the private territory for Anthony since he was the oldest. Theresa had her own room, this time with a door on it. The only problem was that to get to her room, she had to go through Ramon and Donald's room. Stephen's room this time was the dining room. She had hoped he would be moving out anyway. He still stayed in between his grandmother's and mother's house.

Cookson Terrace was a small street with just four houses on it. Across from the house was a strange undulating wooded area that was out of place. It was full of trees and when you get to the top there was a big drop in the middle that seemed bottomless. It was secluded and scary yet Theresa use to go up there to sit and write and dream about Michael Jackson. She was looking for a place similar to what Esther had. *Esther was a character in a book of the same name. Esther had been raped and found a secluded space where she would go to write, daydream and talk to God for strength and courage.*

Stephen saw that his sister went up into the woods often. He would watch her take a notebook and walk up the hill. Sometimes he would just follow her up there and hide behind a tree to just watch what she was doing. "These woods are really secluded," he thought, "I could just rape her right here and she wouldn't even know who it was…I could get away with it. She is so into that Michael Jackson fantasy she wouldn't even know what was coming…Nah, I want her to know it was me…otherwise I would have to throw her over that cliff." He visualized making love to his sister. "Yeah, it's about that time. She's seasoned just enough!"

Hmm, but what a perfect place he thought, to take someone else, into the woods, right by our house.

It was a hot and humid July morning when the Boston Herald headlines reported:

"A small six year old colored girl, on her way home from the MDC Pool was brutally raped. It is said she was taken to a wooded area unknown to her. She was found walking naked along Blue Hill Avenue in Mattapan, with a sock in her mouth and some lollipops in her hand."

Last night, Theresa saw her brother coming out of the Woods on Cookson Terrace. His clothes were disheveled, his eyes were dazed and he had a smirk on his face. He had just planted another weed inside the stomach of yet another child victim.

Theresa had noticed too, the family of skunks that were walking across the road and into their yard.

Chapter Twenty-Nine

Saturdays mornings at 21 Cookson Terrace were often filled with the smell of bacon and eggs and the sound of the Jackson Five cartoon.

It wasn't just Theresa but the entire family that enjoyed watching it to hear which song would be sung. And they could barely wait to see the Alphabet Cereal commercial that the Jackson Five were in... *"What has five heads, ten legs, and eleven alphabets? You don't know it's us the Jackson 5...and that's no jive!"*

Theresa had wide smiles whenever she saw Michael Jackson on television. Stephen was very aggravated by it all. His sister belonged to him. He knew nothing happened between her and Michael Jackson when she flew to Las Vegas to meet him for her sixteenth birthday. Ended up they were both shy and Michael was very religious. He wasn't the typical entertainer who hopped into bed with just any girl and Theresa was just like him in that respect and was still a virgin.

On the Saturday of June 5, 1976, the day of Theresa's graduation from Boston Technical High School, none of her brothers wanted to attend. She was very disappointed. She was getting an award that day.

Her two younger brothers decided to go swimming instead and while Ramon was practicing his diving for an upcoming diving meet, he miscalculated the jump and hit the diving board breaking both of his arms.

With both arms in full cast, Ramon had no hands to use to wipe his ass when he went to the bathroom. Stephen found a sick excitement in Ramon's disability and shame. He enjoyed it every time his little brother had to go to the bathroom, Stephen was there to wipe Ramon's ass or pull out and hold his penis for him when he needed to urinate.

"At least after moving to Cookson Theresa no longer had two hundred and ten pictures of Michael Jackson on her wall. And then she goes off and flies to Las Vegas to meet him for her sixteenth birthday. She didn't do anything with him, she was still a virgin. She use to have a crush on Roderick, but I put a stop to that. He's my best friend now. Ha ha ha."- Stephen, the Man in the Woods

Chapter Thirty

12 Mamelon Circle (1976)

Just after Theresa graduated from High School, Rosetta purchased another home a block away from 21 Cookson Terrace. It was a really nice duplex, in which each unit contained two bedrooms and although there wasn't enough room for all of them, Rosetta decided to move them into one of the two bedroom units.

Theresa was given one bedroom and Rosetta had the other and she had the boys build out the basement to add two bedrooms for them, sort of like their own place. Stephen however, continued sleeping on the couch. His pattern hadn't changed.

At seventeen, Theresa's disdain for her mother, made her move out. She had graduated from high school, attended Boston Business School and started a job working full time with a lot of overtime. Her mother was constantly saying that she needed to get out and treated her badly. Although her boys didn't even work and did nothing all day long, Rosetta picked on Theresa constantly.

Stephen missed her, but Theresa didn't want him over at her apartment at all. At least she seemed safe in the high rise she moved into. There was a doorman there for security. Stephen decided to let go of her for a little while and joined the Marines.

At some point each of Rosetta boys were in one branch of the service. Anthony had been in the Navy; Donald the Army, Ramon was in the Air Force and Stephen as mentioned, joined the Marines. He was sent to Parris Island, South Carolina. He was twenty years old.

Chapter Thirty-One

Parris Island (Spring, 1977)

The entrance to the U.S. Marines Recruit Depot at Parris Island, South Carolina, gives the impression of being very inviting. Palms trees surround the bright red entrance sign. It gives one a sense of belonging there. "Yeah," Stephen thought to himself as the bus drove through the gates, *"I belong here...one of the few, the proud...yeah a marine. That's me."*

It was, however, a short lived thought and relationship that Stephen had with the Marines.

They shaved his head the first day he arrived. He was angry about that. Stephen was simply not a person who took orders well.

During the first two weeks of basic training, two recruits had been killed. Stephen believed it was done on purpose. He didn't like being awakened at 4 a.m. with some damn drill sergeant interrupting his sleep by slamming doors and yelling "GOOD MORNING LADIES ...DROP YOUR COCKS AND GRAB YOUR SOCKS!"

He felt he wasn't given any food to eat. Though trained in martial arts, and thought to be very disciplined, he merely refused to take orders. He asked to get out.

"I want out," he told the Sergeant.

"Well you don't just get out! You signed on for this. And address me as Drill Sergeant."

"Yeah right Sir," Stephen said sarcastically then continued, "I didn't sign on to be killed by my own people. You guys took a kid out there and told him to swim and he drowned and you guys just let him. He didn't know how to swim. You aren't going to kill me. No way. Then they dragged that other kid by the ankles and he had some kind of attack and died. You people killed him. I saw it with my own eyes." Stephen continued belligerently.

"Look Private Gonsalves, I am going to send you for psychological counseling. I am tired of this constant banter."

The Sergeant had two Privates escort Stephen to the Medical barracks'. As he watched him being escorted, he wondered too, how quickly he could get him the hell out of here without a scandal. "Damn, he would have made a great Marine, the crazy bastard."

145

He seems sane, the Marine psychiatrist thought, but there also seems to be some kind of screw loose ... *hmm* no real emotion.

"Well Private Gonsalves, not cutting it huh?"

"I am not going to be killed by my own people," he stated factually, "That's for sure."

"Come on Private Gonsalves, you are a martial artist. You can cut this mustard. What's the problem?"

"They kill people here. We are supposed to go after the enemy. That's what I signed on for. Figured I could kill a few people legally. Instead they try to kill you here, my own people. They're not getting me. I want out."

"Sounds a little paranoid to me Private Gonsalves," said the doctor, fully aware of the two recent death incidences on the base. They were unfortunate mishaps that happen from time to time. The doctor shook off the thought.

"Well, I'll tell you what then, I am really good on the marksmanship field. Great with guns," Stephen responded with calm conviction, "and as soon as you all give me some bullets, I am going to shoot everyone in here! Do some real damage. Take out as many as I can before I go."

Orders were written up immediately for his release. 'Private Gonsalves unfit for military service – psychological medical discharge.' Ship him home as quickly as possible.

Chapter Thirty-Two

When Stephen arrived back to Boston, he went straight back to his mother's house. He got a job at the Franklin Park Zoo, cleaning up behind the animals. He didn't fear any of the animals and actually made a friend with what was suppose to be one of the most fearsome Gorillas in the United States. He didn't like the work, but it drew him to the site where many children visited and he was very curious about the animals. He would watch them for hours. He studied them. He wondered who were the uncivilized, us or them. He continuously broke the rules by bringing them a variety of foods and he often left a gate open hoping one of the animals would escape. Finally they fired him.

In 1980, with just a GED, Stephen somehow managed to get a job at Stonehill College, a small Catholic college just outside of Boston in Easton, MA, where he counseled students that were sent from the Upward Bound Program for troubled teens. He also taught Karate workshops.

But the thing he enjoyed the most was when he was the Director of the schools Talent Show. It was the power and the control he felt in deciding what kids would be able to perform. Everyone did favors for him to get into the show. He sat through the auditions feeling like a big shot, with his arms folded as each student performed. Each performance he felt was just for him.

When the show turned out to be a huge success, Stephen decided he wanted to be a star! He was patted on the back. He was given all kinds of kudos and even a mention in Stonehill College's student run newspaper, The Summit. He was the center of attention for at least a week. He wasn't missing his sister at the moment.

Chapter Thirty-Three

Theresa was living in California now. She had moved there in 1979 after being encouraged by Michael Jackson. Stephen hated the distance and still couldn't understand what he felt was an unnatural attachment she had toward this scrawny singer.

In April of 1980, the Gonsalves kids received a call. Their Grandmother Olivia Fisher was dead. Their father Ronald had been the one who called Theresa.

"What are you doing?" he asked.

"Sleeping ..." she told him groggily. She had been out partying the night before and hadn't gotten in until six a.m. It was just now turning eight a.m. on that Saturday morning.

"Well, I have something to tell you. Your grandmother died, now go back to sleep."

Out of any person in the world, her grandmother was the most special to her. She was devastated by the news and broke down.

"What kind of way was that for a father to tell his daughter that her grandmother had died?" Theresa cried to her friend Lorraine who was visiting her at the time.

Theresa had spent all of her free time with her grandmother. For years it was Theresa who took her grandmother Xmas shopping for all of her other twenty-three grandkids. It was her grandmother who allowed her to read sex books and talked to her about sex. It was her grandmother who loved having her around.

Her phone rang again. It was Stephen. "They killed our grandmother Theresa. They killed her," he cried.

"What are you talking about they killed her? How did she die?"

"Dad killed her. He pushed her and she had a heart attack. It was him and Uncle Joseph. They were fighting with some Puerto Rican dudes because they were sitting on dad's raggedy old jacked up car and Grandma went outside to stop it and Dad or Uncle Joseph pushed her. I don't know which one did it but I blame them both. She had at least another good five years. They killed her and I'll never forgive them for that."

151

That was the first time in her life that Theresa had ever heard her brother reveal sadness and dismay or better yet any kind of real feelings at all.

Grandma was 82 years old. Theresa felt guilt at having moved from Boston and leaving her in what ended up being Grandma's final year. Stephen actually wanted to kill their father.

After Grandma died, Stephen felt totally alone in the world. She had been the only one who had truly shown him love or any kind of true honest attention.

Yet now without his grandmother and after being made to feel like a star, through his small but unique opportunity at Stonehill College, Stephen decided he wanted to pursue his dream to become a star.

He decided he truly needed to be in New York.

Chapter Thirty-Four

Stephen went, however, to *Syracuse* New York and not Manhattan where most wannabe stars tried to get that lucky break.

He was actually chasing after the one girl he claimed to love in high school, Gayla Thomas. He never found her there but decided to stay.

Still saddened and despondent over his grandmother's death, Stephen started hanging out at the neighborhood bar drinking beer. It was there he met Jackie. She offered to buy him a drink. He took the drink of course. Why wouldn't he? It was free.

Jackie Johnson was an old drunk of a woman, constantly with a cigarette stuck hanging out of her mouth. Her hair was thin and graying and her dark brown skin was never smoothed with lotion, so quite often she looked very ashy. Her lips were cracked from the dryness of the winters. A little bit of Vaseline would have helped. She was forty-two but looked much older, while Stephen was simply twenty-five years old. She had a twenty year old daughter, Phyllis, who was following in her mothers footsteps, continuing the welfare cycle with three kids from three different fathers.

Stephen moved in with Jackie after two weeks. She had been on the verge of eviction from her apartment, but was giving the management a run for their money...the money she sure wasn't going to ever pay them. Her apartment was old and there were plenty of repairs that needed to be made. It was infested with mice and cockroaches.

She was tired of fighting with the management and going back and forth to court. She had been with Stephen for two weeks, probably longer than she had been with any man in more than eight years. She felt he was pretty cool and figured she didn't really have anything to lose. He had enough money to pay the rent and he just wanted to bring a cat. Jackie liked cats.

Their relationship was wreaked with havoc. Stephen liked things calm and serene. He didn't like anyone bothering him. With her everything was a problem. She was a thief. She smoked a lot of weed. But he didn't know how to get rid of her.

One evening, without warning, while Jackie and Stephen were walking out of the corner liquor store, Jackie started a fight with some small time gangster who needed to complete an initiation task of killing someone.

She wasn't their victim of choice, but she had accused him of trying to steal her two quart bottle of Colt 45 and her half quart of vodka.

"Fuck you," the gang member told her, "Ain't no one trying to steal your shit."

"You, better watch the fuck how you talk to me you little punk ass," she slobbered walking away as she spit down towards his direction. Instantly following that act, gunshots rang out after the two of them. Stephen grabbed Jackie, practically dragging her as they ducked and dodged bullets.

He needed to take the heat off of them. There had been too many close calls with this crazy woman. He wasn't afraid to die, but he sure wasn't willing to die for her. They began running and this time, they ran all the way to Boston and straight to his mama's house. "Perfect timing," thought Stephen, "I get to see my sister. Maybe now she's ready. I'm sure she's ripe."

Rosetta had been anxiously awaiting the arrival of her only daughter, Theresa, who was four months pregnant with her first son. Her daughter seldom reached out to her as Rosetta had never been a real mother to her. Rosetta felt she needed to be there for her now to make up for the way she had treated her in the past.

In her mind, and as she explained to Theresa, she had treated her badly to make her independent enough to never have to depend solely on any man. While she had succeeded in accomplishing that goal, in her heart, Rosetta realized she had totally neglected the girl.

What Rosetta hadn't anticipated was Stephen and this older woman who came to her house to shamelessly live off of her generosity.

Jackie was loud and rude and refused to help out around the house. They spent most of their time in the refurbished basement. After hearing how vulgar Jackie had been towards her mother, when Theresa arrived, she didn't hesitate to tell Jackie to get out of her mother's house. Jackie didn't care that Theresa was four months pregnant when the two of them got into a fist fight.

"Stephen, get your sorry ass girlfriend and get her the hell out of my house!" Rosetta shouted as she broke up the fight.

"Damn it Jackie. Wherever you go, you cause problems." Stephen yelled at her. He had truly had enough.

Rosetta gave him money for two train tickets and they headed back to Syracuse. Jackie went back to her apartment. Stephen headed to the other side of town as far away as he could get from her in the same city. He was done with her. The cat had liked her. He left the cat.

"Yeah, Jackie, she was crazy. She started all kind of trouble. At first it was okay because I just needed a place to stay. But she just would never shut up. I got into all kind of fights because of her, a couple of gun fights too." - Stephen

Chapter Thirty-Five

311 Irving, Apt 4

Stephen wasn't able to find work right away when he arrived back in Syracuse so he often slept in homeless shelters or in some park or subway. One of the workers at the shelter told him that he could apply for general relief along with food stamps.

When he went to social services, he was given general relief, food stamps and set him up for a job interview at a state funded daycare center.

He had no experience at a daycare, but the program was open to the men or women who applied for general relief. Instead of letting them live off the state, why not give them a job in a state funded program with state children.

Since he did not have any police records or any verifiable offenses that would affect his working there, he was hired immediately. "This is the perfect job for me," Stephen said joyfully.

With his job established, food stamps, and two paychecks in the bank, Stephen got an apartment. 311 Irving Avenue housed 33 units. The rent was cheap, the place barely passing city code. Stephen moved into Apartment 4. The entrance into the building smelled as rancid as an outhouse, by the front door because often homeless drunks would use the stairway as their toilet.

But 311 Irving Ave was just two blocks from the daycare. This allowed Stephen to walk to work or ride his bike. His apartment was a small one bedroom unit.

Stephen furnished his place with mixed matched items that were put out for trash or from the goodwill stores. He didn't need much. Food stamps covered his eating needs.

But he felt he was missing something and discovered it one day as he stumbled upon three abandoned kittens near the sewer drain. He took all three of them in. The one he named Trixie became his favorite. She seemed to love him.

In the beginning he was often alone in his apartment. But then the neighborhood kids starting playing hide and go seek and using the buildings stairway as a place to hide. He began playing little games with them. They liked him a lot.

Stephen genuinely loved the children at the daycare and all the kids loved Stephen too. The rapport he had with the children was easily seen by the parents. The moms saw him as an answer to their prayers for there was finally a man that was willing to spend quality time with their children and be the role model that they had been hoping would come along.

Very often on Saturday afternoon and evenings, mothers, particularly single mothers, would drop their children off with Stephen. Timmy was a regular. At the age of six, he was a scrawny little white boy who looked about four years old. He was underweight at only 48lbs and was just forty-five inches tall. Before he started going to Stephen's place, his clothes were always tattered, dirty and a faint sewage smell followed him in every direction. Stephen spent whatever money he had and bought him new clothes. He even bought him some LA Gears!

Timmy was very fond of Stephen and thought of him as if he were his real dad. He had met his real dad a couple of times, but Stephen seemed more like a father to him. He wanted to call him daddy, but Stephen hadn't said it was okay yet. Stephen treated him like he was his own son, teaching him proper etiquette like washing his hands after using the toilet and saying thanks to God before eating food.

For almost two years, Stephen took Timmy and some of the other children lots of places. It didn't matter if it was a little girl or a little boy. What mattered to him was that they were no older than nine years old.

The state funded daycare center knew that Stephen had outside relationships with the children. It was allowed because they paid so little, they agreed it was okay for the day care teachers to make money on the side by babysitting for the parents. The parents, however, were made to sign a disclaimer.

Stephen took the kids to the zoo. They hung out at the park, the movie theater. He even taught them how to roller skate.

He would tickle them and blow fart noises on their stomachs and they would laugh hysterically. He spent plenty of time doing what he called loving them when he was actually playing a slow game of seduction.

When the time was right and he knew exactly when that moment was, he began kissing and fondling each child that he had prepped as his prey, more boys than girls. He had found that the boys were less likely to tell anyone and for some reason to him, they always seemed softer to the touch.

He knew that each child had issues at home and wanted his attention. And to him, each of the children, Jeremy, Elaine, Bianca, John and Timmy, enjoyed the pleasure he gave them when he fondled them, kissed them or played with their genitals. He didn't come on full force right away. He had to play it just right.

But when he did, Stephen still had to make sure that the children wouldn't tell and would keep happily coming back. *"How would your mother feel if she knew that we did this?"* he would ask. Subsequently he would tell them, *"You started it first. You liked having me do those things. It would be sad if you told your mother. It might make her kill herself or something."*

That line had always worked. The children felt guilt and shame especially knowing that they themselves had actually felt sexual enjoyment, something they didn't understand. While deep down they knew it was wrong they were not sure why because all they knew was that it felt good. Guilty pleasure alone would make them keep the secret to themselves.

Timmy was one of Stephen's favorites. He was with Stephen the most. In 1986, Timmy was just turning seven years old. His mother had been strung out on crack and was struggling to get back on her feet. She would often leave him with Stephen for days at a time. She wasn't trying very hard.

One early afternoon while out at the movies Timmy who had a weak bladder, had wet his pants and since they were close to Stephen's brother Donald's apartment, Stephen decided it would be better to take him there to clean him up then to have him walking feeling embarrassed about a big stain on his pants.

Donald had been surprised to see Stephen had a kid with him. Yes, he had seen him plenty of times with a kid or two before. But he never imagined he would bring one to his house. Donald thought he was hallucinating. He was strung out on crack and whatever drug he could get his hands on.

Donald's apartment was small but roomy. He was what you could call a functioning drug addict. He hardly had any furniture in his place, but he did have a couch that also functioned as his bed.

Donald drew Timmy a bath and gently bathed him rubbing soap all up and down his body. It was ticklish.
"You're tickling me," Timmy laughed infectiously.
"Ha ha ha," Donald laughed back with wicked intent, "You like that huh?" and continued to playfully wash him. A quick fleeting thought ran through Donald's head, "I wonder how much I could get for this kid?" He quickly let that go because he knew Stephen would literally kill him if he ever tried that with one of his kids. "Shit, he acts like these kids are really his." Yeah, Stephen would track him down and make sure he didn't breathe another day if he remotely attempted the idea.

Stephen was in the kitchen hand washing Timmy's clothes. When he finished he turned on the oven and placed the clothes on the oven door to dry.

They knew it would take some time to dry so they decided to just hang out as Timmy sat with just a towel wrapped around his waist between them on an old tattered beige sofa. They played with the kitten and had some snacks and decided to watch a video. The Wizard of Oz was one of Timmy's favorite movies. Just when the munchkins appeared as Timmy sat comfortably between the two brothers, they both began to gently fondle him and kiss his naked little body.

Even though it sometimes felt nice to him, Timmy didn't like the touching so much, but it pleased Stephen so he endured it. But he wanted to cry when his head was pushed down to Stephen's crotch so he could lick "daddy's lollipop." He didn't want anyone else to see him doing that, especially when the white stuff came out that would make him gag. "Just swallow it!" Stephen had yelled at him. That was the only time he would ever get mad at him but the saltiness of it would make him nauseous and throw up. It took all of Timmy's power to not cry each time. Every so often, he would go into the bathroom and curl up into a ball next to the toilet and silently cry while Stephen slept. He couldn't get the image out of his mind...the curly black pubic hair, the wrinkly look of the freckled penis.

Timmy was particularly disturbed this time more so now than usual because Stephen let his brother watch what was their personal game. The dirty feeling came over him again. With sad eyes and shock, he fought back tears as Stephen started licking and sucking on his small penis. He didn't understand why he felt so sad cause when the white stuff came out it actually felt good to him. But still, it made him feel dirty. He looked up at Donald and Stephen with trepidation, a look that they both interpreted as enjoyment.

He studied Donald's face and noticed that he had a look that his mother often had after doing drugs. He was extremely thin like his mom and was twitching a lot and he had spacey eyes. Sometimes his eyes would just close and then he would seemingly wake back up. He didn't like Donald's sinister laugh.

But when he looked at Stephen, he saw how much happiness it brought to him and Timmy wouldn't complain. He didn't want to lose his daddy, so he just did whatever Stephen wanted him to do. He had gotten use to it.

Chapter Thirty-Six

The parents continued to trust Stephen with their children. After all, they thought, he had found himself a girlfriend and the kids never complained about anything. They all seemed just fine. Unbeknownst to the parents, a woman lived with him, but he didn't exactly consider her his girlfriend.

Cheryl had been homeless and needed a place to stay. She kept knocking on Stephen's door asking if he wanted company and after telling her no four or five times, he finally caved in and opened up his place to her.

Cheryl was a tall, lanky woman, with unruly shoulder length chestnut brown hair. She was a shade of ceramic pasty white. Her eyes were brown, but tired. Her small lips housed brown decaying teeth but she was always smiling. She was a heavy smoker and drank a lot of beer and played the lottery. She worked at Store 24. She didn't know much about Stephen. She did know she couldn't stand all the cats but it was a place to stay and she was grateful for that. It beat sleeping outside on some park bench in the cold.

Sex between them was just something to do. At times she feared him, especially after she gave him syphilis. She had slept with a variety of men mostly just to keep warm or sometimes for a spare buck or two.

Stephen's behavior was odd. At times she feared him. Although he had never hit her, he would seem violent and at other times so gentle and loving. But she became strangely attracted to him as time passed by.

She considered them an item. He thought she was dumb and didn't really like her. He had given her a place to stay and simply promised her that he would never physically hurt her.

After living with him for eight months, Cheryl discovered she was pregnant. She had always been irregular and didn't expect it. She knew how much Stephen loved children and although she hadn't seen the children around the apartment a lot she had seen signs of their being there. She also had noticed that he bought a lot of children's clothing and toys. Yet, she was rarely there when the children came by.

"Hey Stephen, I have some wonderful news!" Cheryl told him flatly with no excitement in her voice.

"Oh yeah, what's that?" he questioned with blatant disinterest.

Cheryl smiled at him, took his dirty yellow big stubby fingered hand and put it on her stomach.

"I am pregnant. We are going to have a baby!"

The room fell completely silent and for a full two minutes Stephen just stood there, his hand still on her stomach. He smirked, looked directly in her eyes, and then suddenly, unexpectedly spit a big loogie in her face.

Shock could hardly describe her reaction as she instantly spit right back in his. He grabbed her by her shoulders and remembering his promise, placed her gently, but firmly down on to the floor.

"Get out! I don't want to hear from you again," he told her, "I only expect to hear from you if I hit the lottery or something, because I'm sure you'd be looking for child support then."

Cheryl, in absolute disbelief, packed her clothes and left. He never heard from her again and never found out if he was a father or not.

"Timmy was one of the first ones. He use to just stand outside my window until I invited him. Cheryl didn't like that at all. I had him on one side of the house and had her on the other side. I wanted to adopt him so I could keep him." – Stephen, aka The Man in the Woods

Chapter Thirty-Seven

In 1982, Theresa gave birth to her son Todd who was the key to the song Billie Jean which Michael Jackson wrote about her. After she and Michael met in 1976, they had stayed friends. Calls from her brother Stephen began coming in daily from New York.

Initially she didn't mind receiving his calls because the distance between them was three thousand miles. She never forgot the fear he had instilled in her when she had turned fifteen. Eventually his calls started to become disturbing.

"Theresa, I want to marry you," Stephen told her.

"What's wrong with you?" she responded with disgust. "I am your sister. That is just sick. We have the same mother and father. Are you crazy?"

"Well, in Bible days, brothers and sisters got married," he declared knowledgeably as if he had been studying the Bible.

"Well I certainly wouldn't want to marry my damn brother," Theresa yelled as she slammed down the phone.

But he was persistent. He continued to call her over and over and over. She became more afraid because he wouldn't stop and didn't know if he would just show up in California at her apartment. She called their mother.

"Mummy...What the hell is wrong with your son? Stephen keeps calling up here asking me to marry him," Theresa called screaming at her mother in an accusing tone as if to say, *you created this monster now do something about him.*

Her mother was disturbed herself, as Stephen had been calling her with the same bullshit. But she was not going to let her daughter be harassed. She called Stephen and demanded that he leave Theresa alone.

When her brother called Theresa the next time, it was a different conversation.

"Gret," that was the nickname that all of her brothers called her. "I was just playing with you about marrying me. I won't ask you anymore," he told her. "Besides, I really want to marry Rhonda. She's still a virgin. You have a kid already."

Rhonda was their half sister. Theresa worried about her, but figured it was out of her hands now. She had her son Todd to think about. Stephen was in Syracuse, New

York and Rhonda was in Boston. She was out of harms way for the moment as was Theresa.

Chapter Thirty-Eight

Syracuse 1987

The sound of the first morning train startled Timmy's mother. Caitlyn Allen awoke early Friday morning lying face down in a puddle of water next to a water gutter on Canal Street under the graffitied railroad tracks. Her hand reached down as she searched the ground and then her pockets for her stash. She couldn't find it and she was coming down from her high. She instantly and reflexively started scratching. She was broke and wanted her crack, something that she relied on to sustain her daily life.

It took a few minutes for Caitlyn to realize that she was partially dressed wearing only a bra and threadbare leggings. It was January, she was freezing. She stood up with a wobble. Her head ached. She didn't remember how she ended up in the puddle and didn't really want to remember. This was just another episode in the series of events that had clouded her life for the last six years. She realized she was only two blocks from her apartment and began limping home.

The front door to her apartment was unlocked. For the first time in days Caitlyn wondered where Timmy was. "Did I leave him with the daycare teacher again?" she wondered scratching her head. She walked in and looked around her apartment. She spotted Timmy on the floor. He was asleep next to the rusty radiator under the window of their living room. She walked over and covered him with the blanket he had kicked off.

Their apartment was a small one bedroom. She was on welfare with subsidized rent and food stamps that she often traded for drugs. By claiming to be taking business classes she was able to get free daycare for Timmy for after school hours. She felt lucky that Stephen, Timmy's favorite daycare teacher, took good care of Timmy as if he was his real father. She never paid him. Hell, he never asked her to.

Caitlyn and Timmy didn't have much furniture. She didn't feel like she needed anything other than the powdered substance that sustained her.

On her way to the bathroom, Caitlyn glanced at the picture of herself and Timmy that they had hung on the wall when he was five years old. She sighed. Caitlyn walked into her bathroom and turned on the shower. She was still craving the rush from the crack cocaine that talked to her soul. She couldn't describe the euphoric, exhilarating feeling it gave her. All Caitlyn knew was that she was anxious to get some more. As she took off what little clothes she had on, she caught a glance of herself in the mirror.

She stopped frozen for twenty seconds as she saw herself as she really was. She was appalled at what she saw … an extremely thin girl who looked like she was no younger than thirty-eight years old. Caitlyn had just turned twenty-six. She had Timmy when she was sixteen. His father had left some time ago. She could barely remember who he was or what he looked like, let alone his name. Her eyes were sullen with sunken dark circles. Her hair greasy and straight was disheveled all over her head. It was so dirty she couldn't even tell what color it actually was.

Caitlyn didn't get in the shower. She ran in the living room and woke up Timmy. She looked in his face. She wanted to scream. Anxiety was setting in. She felt the walls beginning to close in on her.

"Hi baby," she said softly trying to maintain some sensibility, sitting down on the floor beside him.

"Mom, where have you been? Are you okay?" he asked fuzzily in a whisper, as he wiped his eyes with fisted hands.

Caitlyn stared at her son. His eyes looked sad. They looked so very sad. She put her boney arms around him and held him for a long time.

"I miss you mommy."

She let him go, jumped up and ran into the kitchen and like a mad woman started searching the cabinet drawers. She found matches; she found receipts from the daycare center; she found little drawings Timmy had made at some stage or another in his life, she couldn't remember, until finally she found what she had been looking for …her mother's phone number.

Caitlyn prayed silently, yet nervously to God for three things: "God, please let this number be the same; God please let my telephone still be working; and Lord please help me get off these drugs."

Her phone was still on. She dialed the number. She clutched the phone tightly against her right ear. It rang four times before her mother answered. It had seemed an eternity.

"Mother, I need help …" Caitlyn whispered softly into the phone as she dropped to her knees, "I need to get off these drugs. His eyes, mother … Timmy's *eyes* … they are so sad mom. They are so sad."

Chapter Thirty-Nine

Rosetta Frye at 53 was still very sexy. She still maintained her petite size five from her teen years. The continuous daily drinking of a complete six pack of beer had however caused her to begin to develop a beer belly.

Rosetta had been divorced from her second husband for over twenty five years. She had enjoyed a variety of many lovers after her second divorce in 1965. However, there were two men that she loved but could never have. They were Cortland Ballard and Preston Williams.

Besides Rosetta, the two men shared another common bond. They were both detectives in the Boston Police Department. Cortland an average height Black man, with medium brown skin color was, unfortunately, a married man. If you could describe someone as sexy, yet *non-descript* with a slightly large head that would sum up Cortland. Rosetta knew he would stay in his marriage. He would simply come over for occasional casual sex.

Preston at the time was a legendary player. Women were easily accessible to him, so why settle down. He was tall, Hershey chocolate brown skin, a well groomed mustache with a slight receding hairline. Preston was kind of a cross between Jeffrey Osborne and Garrett Morrison. When in uniform, women couldn't keep their hands off of him.

Rosetta was one of them. Their relationship, or as much of a relationship she could get from him, was based on lust. While he professed to love her, it was never enough to make it a committtable relationship.

Many a nights though, Rosetta would get dressed up in one of her many sexy outfits and go to Lane's Lounge in hopes of seeing him there. And if he wasn't there she always managed to find some man to take home with her. Men were simply a comfort to her.

Sometime in 1972, Rosetta had met Ed Cruse. Ed Cruse was a carpenter who fell very hard for Rosetta. He became an integral part of her life as he tried for years to be what she wanted in a man.

The problem … he was just too nice. He was a classic case of the nice guy finishing last. Two years later, after falling in love with her and her kids, came the final straw.

He saw her out at a bar with another man and he flipped. She saw Ed from across the bar. Their eyes met. But she still continued with her flirtatious ways. When he saw her leave alone, he followed her home. He was surprised at how well she drove after having numerous drinks. She seldom drove her blue and white classic Cutlass Supreme. She even had her son drive when she needed to run her errands and she took the bus to work. Nevertheless, when she went out at night she drove. "I drive better when I am drunk," she often told her kids.

Although Rosetta was high as hell, she had felt Ed's presence and knew he was behind her when she walked in the door.

"What the fuck do you think you were doing?" he yelled in her face, spit spraying from his mouth.

They were still living at 21 Cookson Terrace at the time and Stephen was lying on the couch in the living room, two rooms over from the kitchen and heard Ed yelling at her. Theresa was spending the night at her friend Lorraine's house and Ramon and Donald were upstairs asleep. Stephen just laid there because all the kids knew Ed was a wuss where their mother was concerned and felt he wouldn't do anything to hurt her.

"Woman don't you know that I love you? You just slapped me in the face being in that club throwing yourself at that guy!"

"Well I don't love you," Rosetta loudly retorted, her words slurring from liquor. When Rosetta was drunk, she was also very honest. "I told you before that you were just wasting your time, that I would never love you, but you wouldn't leave...You can't make me love you." Rosetta put a great deal of emphasis on that last statement and Ed, after all these years, let out his anger.

He reached out and slapped her across her face so hard that it made his hand ache. He grabbed her and was about to push her down on the ground, but when Stephen had heard the loud slap, he jumped off the couch and ran into the kitchen where they were standing and grabbed Ed into a chokehold.

"Let go of me Stephen," Ed yelled out.

"If you put your hands on my mother again, you won't have any life left in you. I will take you out," he replied calmly while slowly releasing him from such a tight grip, being sure not to let him go. He knew his mother had used Ed for a long time but still wasn't going to tolerate any man physically hurting her.

Ed knew that Stephen was a martial arts expert and could easily kill him and probably get away with it.

"Let him go now Stephen," his mother ordered sympathetically. He kept his hold a moment longer and then let go, pushing him as he did.

"Get the hell out of my house," was the last words she said to him.

Ed regained his composure, rubbing his hand around his neck to soothe the pain he received during the chokehold Stephen had on him. He looked directly at Rosetta.

"I am sorry I ever loved you." She knew it was the end simply because she chose to no longer be a victim of any man's abuse.

Ed's life from then on was never the same. Alcohol became his wife. Real women could no longer soothe him as much as a good ole bottle of whiskey could. His work suffered and his mind wandered.

His next girlfriend Stephanie became prey to Rosetta's leftovers when Ed, in one of his drunken stupors, took a blow torch to thaw some frozen pipes in her basement during the winter's cold and instead blew up her house. Fortunately no one was hurt, but Stephanie's home was completely destroyed.

Chapter Forty

No matter how many men had been in her bed, Rosetta continued for years to hold that burning torch for Preston.

Rosetta had spoken to Preston on the phone earlier Saturday afternoon and he agreed to meet her at The Carousel Lounge on Columbia Road later that evening. It had been a while since he saw her, so he was just going to sneak off of his shift and have a couple of drinks with her. He had missed her.

Work had been dragging Preston down. He felt he was being harassed and mistreated by his underlings. He was considered quite militaristic and didn't get along well with individuals that didn't meet his required standards. He was pretty tough on the men. He wanted to make them into better police officers.

Instead several officers felt picked on, like little sissies and became so angered that two officers took yellow police tape, used for crowd control, and tied it into a noose. They took the noose shaped tape and hung the noose over

185

Preston's parked patrol motorcycle in the police parking garage. Preston took it as a threat. When the officers were caught, they called it a prank.

In later years after continuing incidents, when Preston filed a discrimination suit against the city of Boston, the judge would say, "the noose incident was particularly troubling and came close to the type of event that *might* underline a viable hostile work environment." And with that the case was dismissed.

Once again Blacks in Boston were reminded that progress in racial diversity was far behind and that blatant racist acts were still being thrown right in their faces.

Meeting Rosetta that evening would be a relief for him. She had been the one constant woman who remained in his life. He just wasn't ready to settle down and really didn't want to put her life in danger with his line of work, especially battling with his co-workers as well as the bad guys. Maybe later he thought.

Rosetta always made him smile. She always made him relax. He knew what she wanted from him, but yet she never made any demands. This evening wasn't any different. Their conversation was just small talk and they had two drinks. After a little over an hour, he had to get back on duty. He left her with a long passionate kiss, indicating more to come at a later time.

Rosetta sat smiling, having one last drink and smoking another cigarette. Kool's were her cigarette of choice. She had been smoking them for years, since she was sixteen. She felt happy and tired and decided it was time to go home. She hailed a cab as she walked out the club doors. Cabs were always readily available in Boston particularly in front of a club on Columbia Road.

When Rosetta arrived in front of her house, she paid the cab driver and walked up the stairs. The house was quiet but her son Stephen was visiting from New York. She was anxious for him to leave.

Stephen was in his usual position asleep on her sofa with blankets completely covering his entire body including his head. The living room reeked of his body odor. That smell also had been too much of a constant in her life. At least now he was only here temporarily.

Rosetta was a little tipsy. She had one drink too many, but she hadn't gotten as drunk as she normally did. She was in a great mood but the bed was calling her name.

She loved sleeping in the nude especially after a night out. She closed her bedroom door all the way. Normally she would leave it ajar when she was home alone. She took her clothes off, leaving them in a pile on the floor next to her bed and got under the covers. She put her head on her soft goose down pillow and as soon as she did a smile covered her face. Her thoughts were of Preston as she drifted off into a deep alcohol induced sleep.

Rosetta didn't hear her bedroom door open, nor did she hear her son enter her room. So she didn't sense Stephen, naked and shadowing over her. In fact, she didn't even stir until she felt him get into her bed.

At first she was hazy and in a dreamlike state. But when she realized it was her son in the bed right beside her and that he was naked, instant panic awakened her fully. "What the hell are you doing Stephen?" she yelled at him as she tried to get out of the bed. He grabbed her and held her down. She tried fighting him, but her strength was no match for his. She did everything she could, she scratched him, she bit him, but to no avail. He simply held her down and remained silent, showing no signs of pain or weakening.

When Stephen entered inside his mother the ecstasy he felt was surreal. He had thought about this for years, just as he had thought about making love to his sister Theresa. Though his mother's vagina was dry and unwelcoming, he found it extremely warm and wet. He felt engulfed as if he was back in the womb where his life had begun.

"Back into the womb. Back inside my mummy. I need to start all over Mother. I need to start all over." Stephen whispered, mumbling in her ear. He bent over to suck her breast. "You never gave me any milk mother. Why didn't you give me any milk?" he asked, his voice a whiny babyish squeal. He squeezed her nipples expecting sweet breast milk to squirt out.

Rosetta lay there unable to move, barely able to breathe. The solidity of his body weighing her down was smothering.

When he finally ejaculated, he lied next to her face down almost spread eagle as his heavy arm slumped over her waist. Stephen fell asleep quickly. Unbelievably his sleep was calm and deep. She wasn't sure what else to expect. The horror of it all encompassed her. She blacked in and out of consciousness. She had feared this child she had birthed since the day he was born. She had always considered him the son of Satan.

When she finally was able to awake, the shame of it all held on to her mental state, keeping her in a frozen position. She laid there, on her back, her eyes staring at the ceiling. The house was silent. When the sun light flooded her room, she finally found the strength to get up. She glanced into the living room. She knew he was gone, but she just wanted to be sure.

Her whole body shook as she stumbled into the bathroom barely making it in time to bring up all the vile she felt in her body. She turned on the shower. She sank into the tub and balled up in a fetal position. She couldn't cry. She didn't make a sound. Her spirit was dead, killed by her own demonic son. She would block this out. She wouldn't forget. She would tell no one. But she never wanted to see him again.

Stephen went back to Syracuse. He had no regrets, only justification. "In Bible days they did it, so why can't I."

He had just planted a dead weed in yet and still another victim. This time the victim was his mother.

"Why are you asking me what I did to mummy? I didn't do anything to her. Mummy didn't want to see me when she was dying. I don't know why but Dad kept telling me she didn't want me to come yet. And then it was too late.

I didn't do anything to her. Everyone is afraid of me. Even Mummy." – Stephen aka The Man in the Woods

Chapter Forty-One

Timmy's mother's cry for help was heard by her mom. Mary Allen drove up from Richmond, Virginia to bring Caitlyn and Timmy home. Caitlyn's dad had died from pneumonia when she was a baby, so Mary was happy to have her daughter home.

While Timmy's life became more normalized, his heart still ached for Stephen. He had been torn between loving him and loathing him. He had gotten use to the sexual acts and he had accepted that as a part of his life with Stephen. He missed Stephen. He was like the father he had never known and probably would never know.

Caitlyn's mother lived in an affluent neighborhood. The neighbor across the street from them was Sharon and Fenmore Dennison. They didn't have any children of their own. Their house seemed to be out of place in the neighborhood as it stood like a palatial palace. Anyone who passed by would immediately notice the exteriors beautiful blend of stucco and stone. The decorative roof was sure to turn heads. On the inside a twelve foot foyer opened to a column decorated great room with a fireplace and media center. The kitchen had a large multi-level island with a walk-in pantry and the master bedroom had a sitting area with a trio of windows that allowed lots of natural light to flow through.

They were obsessive about maintaining an extremely meticulous lawn and one day, knowing Mary's situation with Caitlyn, Sharon Dennison knocked on the door and asked Mary if her grandson Timmy could come over and mow their lawn on the weekends. They all felt it would give him a chance to grow a little and get away from the sadness of his mother's situation and allow him to make a modest amount of money on his own.

The Dennison's took an ardent liking to Timmy and sometimes paid him one hundred dollars a week. He would take the money and give half to his mom. She told him she was saving it so they could get a home of their own. He thought she was doing better. He had no idea she was using the money for drugs.

In May, 1991, Fenmore Dennison had a massive stroke. It was such a massive stroke that it left him paralyzed from the neck down. His mind had remained sound but he couldn't move any part of his body. Fenmore had a true obsession with sports. He had come to terms with his paralysis but missed his sports a great deal, that is, until Timmy came to mind initiating a grand idea. He had his wife invite Timmy over to visit him. Fenmore couldn't talk. He handed Timmy the sports section of the Sunday paper and tapped on it. At first Timmy was confused. Fenmore tapped on it again, hard, nearly crumpling the newspaper.

"I think he wants you to read it to him," Sharon said smiling.

So Timmy began reading to him every single day, the entire sports section, including the statistics. This helped Timmy better develop his reading skills but also gave life to Fenmore's otherwise immobilized body.

Timmy's mother fought hard to stay off the crack but she kept sliding in and out. She continued to neglect him but he didn't feel it as much as when they were in Syracuse. Besides he had his grandmother and his job with the Dennison's.

Three years after Fenmore had his first stroke, his kidneys began to completely shut down and he knew he didn't have much time left. Dialysis would only keep him alive a little while longer.

"I want Timothy to have a college education. Make sure he gets its," Fenmore was able to communicate to his wife, "Promise me that."

"Of course Fenmore," Sharon promised. They had both come to love Timmy. He became the son they never had.

Fenmore died just as Timmy started his sophomore year in high school. Once Fenmore died, Timmy became plagued by his own behavior.

He started to show he was outwardly gay. He had known he was gay since he was about twelve years old. It was a feeling he had always felt within. It wasn't just because he had enjoyed the time he spent with Stephen. He knew he was different when his friends would try to taunt him to sneak a look at one of their dads' Playboy Magazines. Timmy had found no interest in the women in the magazine at all. But he found himself very excited when he rummaged through Mrs. Dennison's dresser drawers, caressing her silk wear for its softness not its sex appeal, and then stumbled upon her Playgirl Magazines. It also thrilled him when the boys from the basketball team passed by him in their tight shorts, his head always turned.

Tried as he might, he had a hard time hiding his homosexuality. So he decided instead of being afraid of it, he would just embrace it. Sometimes he would dress in drag and be the epitome of the character of Angel from the Broadway movie production of Rent. Timmy continued to have a baby face.

He made it through high school without a great deal of scathing and true to their word, the Dennison's paid his way through college where he majored with a Bachelor Degree in Interior Design. Once he graduated, he decided he had to diffuse the flame. He had to face the world as a man and not a kid in drag. His clients didn't mind that he was gay, but they were uncomfortable with the flamboyancy. People of the world always seemed to feel that gay men were the better designers. It was for that reason his company became a success.

When he opened T-Allen's house of Design, his first big client had been Luther Vandros and from then on his clientele consisted of mostly well known celebrities.

Chapter Forty-Two

15 King Street (Worcester, MA)
April 26, 1991

Joseph Gonsalves was dead. Six months prior to his death, he had sat in the window of his apartment in a drunken stupor and fell backwards out of the window and was paralyzed. He had not touched another little girl after Marie. Not wanting to live in a paraplegic state and since his young wife Marie, whom he had actually truly come to love, had died in 1986 from cancer, Joseph refused to eat until finally he passed away to join her.

Her mother Mary had passed three years earlier than Marie from cirrhosis of the liver. She had continued to drink heavily after Joseph married her daughter. She could never get past the pain, but was determined to stay in his life.

With Joseph dead, another evil had left the planet, unearthing the weeds that had grown in the stomachs of all his unnamed victims.

No one had ever found out about Cherene or that he had been the assailant behind the sorrow he caused the victims and families of so many little girls in the Cape Verde Island of Sao Vicente.

Chapter Forty-Three

In October of 1992, Rosetta was diagnosed with lung cancer. She had smoked packs and packs and packs of Kool cigarettes since she was sixteen years old. The woman smoked like a chimney.

"You have six months with no treatment or one year with treatment," the doctor had told her.

After opting for no treatment, Rosetta called her daughter Theresa and her oldest son Anthony.

"You guys get together and decide what you want to do with the houses," she told them each separately.

She had written a Last Will and Testament distributing everything she had to all of her children equally. She did this so there wouldn't be any problems amongst her kids, with a clause in it stating that any child, who tried to contest the Will, would simply get one dollar.

Three weeks after getting the diagnosis, Rosetta woke up one morning unable to move. She was paralyzed. An ambulance arrived at 12 Mamelon Circle to pick her up.

The golf ball sized cancerous lump had grown and was leaning on her spine causing the paralysis.

The doctors went in to remove it, mostly to give her some comfort. She would never be able to walk again.

Theresa flew to Boston to visit her mother. She took her two year old son Mychal in with her. Seeing her grandson granted Rosetta some last moments of happiness. She wasn't eating her food partly because the medication made her nauseous. She made sure Mychal ate it all. He was there jumping up and down on her bed making her laugh. She was sedated so she didn't feel any pain. Some of her words weren't making sense to Theresa.

"You know they are killing me Theresa. You know they put this cancer in my body. They do that to all Black people you know that. They have been using us as experiments for a long, long time. I don't trust them," Rosetta told her sounding defeated.

Theresa felt her mother was delusional when she started saying such things, but these days you never know. Then out of the blue Rosetta sat up, her arms outstretched and opened as wide as she could open them, and started singing Diana Ross' version of Ain't No Mountain High Enough.

"What the hell is wrong with the world when Diana Ross can just open up her arms with that squeaky ass voice, hair all over her head and sing *♪ahh ahh ahh ahh ♫*... and the world stands up and cheers? She was awful. I can sing better than she can. I should have done that and I would have made a lot of money." She started laughing and Theresa laughed with her.

As Theresa was about to leave her side and head back to Atlanta where she was now living, Rosetta stopped her, "I changed my Will. I gave you 12 Mamelon Circle all for you and gave the boys 21 Cookson Terrace. They were the ones who got most of the money when I refinanced it anyway. I don't know where Ramon and Donald are and why they haven't been here to see me."
"What about Stephen? Has he been here?" Theresa asked already knowing her oldest brother Anthony had been there on a couple of occasions.

Rosetta went silent, pain apparent in her eyes. "I didn't leave him anything she said. I don't even want to see him. I told your father to make sure of that. Speaking of your father, he's not that bad after all. He's been up here to visit me everyday. He'll make sure Stephen doesn't come here to see me. I don't want him here. I don't want him here." Her voice was filled with anxiety, she was shaking.

Theresa didn't have the heart to ask her mother why. She figured he had done something to her that must have upset her and it must have been something really awful. Rosetta, as she lay dying, didn't want to say goodbye to her second oldest son. Yet, she tried to hold on for her younger sons to get there.

"What the hell did he do to mummy?" Theresa wondered.

Chapter Forty-Four

The Wake was set during the hours of five through seven p.m. on a wintry Wednesday evening in March 1993, five days after she died.

Theresa was standing by her casket when Stephen walked in. The bottom half of the casket had been closed. She hadn't seen her brother since 1986. He looked like a bum. They would need to buy him a suit for the funeral, she surmised.

"Who picked out her clothes?" he asked.

"I did."

"Why did you get her a white dress?" Stephen felt it looked to pure.

"It's very pretty. I wanted her to be buried in something pretty."

"Well, what happened to her anyway?"

Theresa looked at her brother flabbergasted.

"What kind of question is that? She had lung cancer. You know that. I told all of you guys that she was dying," Theresa responded referring to her brothers.

"Yeah, well I didn't believe you. I didn't expect her to die that fast. Dad kept telling me she was okay and that she didn't want me to come yet."

"Well I don't know why he told you that when I was telling you she was dying." Her voice was filled with annoyance, but she did remember her mother telling her she really hadn't wanted to say goodbye to him.

Stephen just stared at his mother's body in the coffin.

"She looks so old," he stated emptily. Wanting to see all of her body, Stephen lifted the bottom end of the casket to see the rest of his mother's body. His knees buckled as he was taken aback at what he saw. Instantly he dropped the casket cover causing the casket to shake and almost fall from the table.

Rosetta had died weighing only sixty-five pounds. The ending stages of emphysema had sent her into medical anorexia and the small radiation treatment she received turned her into a mass of nothingness. Her legs weren't really legs. They were merely skeletal bones, sticks.

The horrified look on his face couldn't describe the way he actually felt. Heaviness filled his chest. It was like the wind had been knocked out of him by a hard punch to his gut.

"What *happened* to her?" he asked his sister as he tried to recover from the shock of seeing his mother appearing so ruined.

"The cancer," Theresa responded downheartedly, "It ate her alive." She turned and looked at Stephen, continuing to wonder what he had done so bad that made their mother not want to ever see him again.

As he continued to stare at what was left of her body, a small tight smile formed on his face, as he thought of his last night with her. He hadn't needed to say goodbye, he had said his goodbye that evening.

The cancer had taken her body's shell, yet her soul had long been dead. No one would ever really know that she was actually killed by her son three years earlier when he not only planted weeds in another victim, his mother, he had murdered her spirit. She had been executed by Stephen, just as she had wanted to destroy him at his birth.

Rosetta had spent numerous hours thinking back to the pregnancy. The way her body had tightened in pain, the way she felt sick at the thought of him. How she knew he was evil before she birthed him. She felt it every time he kicked her stomach.

She had thought back to the day she gave birth to him, wishing over and over that she had dropped him into the freezing waters of the Charles River. She would have stopped the evil then. Jail would have been better than allowing this monster to walk the earth. She had a momentary hatred for her brother-in-law, Carl, for following her and stopping her that day. Carl thought he was saving her. Instead he had saved a true child of Satan.

Yes, her son Stephen had killed her soul three years earlier. It was simply her shell that had continued to exist.

Chapter Forty-Five

1626 Jamieson Drive – Virginia Beach, VA
April, 1993

After Rosetta passed away, her four sons decided it would be best for all of them to be together. They felt some sense of camaraderie. Their sister had her own life and didn't want to share in any kind of bond they seemed to be feeling at the moment. She was afraid of them and the elements that came with them. She wanted no part of that scene.

Anthony already lived in Virginia Beach, VA, so it was decided that the other three brothers would move to Virginia and go into business together, opening up a maintenance service. Rosetta had left money for the two younger brothers and Theresa and hadn't left a thing for Stephen.

But Theresa, without knowing why their mother didn't leave anything to Stephen, decided they should take their money and make sure that each of them got an equal amount. Their oldest brother had a policy of his own which he didn't care to share.

The brothers took their money and purchased a town home and invested in a Maintenance Franchise together. Stephen, Donald and Ramon would share the town home.

The townhouse was a beautiful three bedroom piece of real estate that sat five miles from the beach in the Chantal community. It had been in foreclosure and they got it at a great price with no money down.

Stephen had gone back to New York before deciding to move to Virginia Beach with his brothers. His sister told him it was not a wise decision. But when they were all together again at their mother's funeral, he felt an alliance, an alliance that he had never felt with them before especially now that his mother was out the way.

But what any of the siblings didn't know was that Stephen needed a new location. He had worked at the day care for many years "Oooo ... I had me a really good time here," he thought sinisterly to himself. But he knew his moment was up in New York. It was time to take his cats and move on. He had no remorse about what he was doing. He had sensed that the police were closing in on him.

He packed up some of his clothes and was sure to pack the clothing he had taken from each child he loved as a souvenir. But most importantly, he had to carry at least three of his cats, especially Trixie.

The cash he thought he received from his mothers death was in the hands of the oldest sibling.

"Hey, I need you to send me some money for a bus ticket for me and my cats."

"Yeah…right, okay," Anthony said with irritation and sarcasm. "Go to the Greyhound station and your ticket will be there."

It was five days before the ticket was actually at the depot station. Anthony had taken all of the brothers' cash and *invested* it for them. There was no money left as far as he was concerned.

When Stephen, Ramon and Donald moved into their new town home, they were together at last. On their first night they reminisced about their lives. They smoked weed and drank beer. Crack was a common usage for them, but tonight they couldn't find a fix and settled for what they could get.

"Where is our sister at?" Stephen asked, "Why is she not here? I've wanted her for a long time."

Donald and Ramon looked at each other surprised at what they heard and felt it was just the drugs talking or that he simply misspoke. They had always considered him crazy but that was just sick.

"You mean you wanted to see her for a long time," said Ramon correcting him.

"No, I know exactly what I said," Stephen responded.

"Hey man," Donald said, "That's my tree-tree, my little Gretchen-boo," his nicknames for her. "That is just sick man. Just sick!" he said disgustedly. "Did you know my sister use to play badminton with me for hours in the middle of the street at Cookson? Man we would keep that birdie in the air for hours at a time too. Yeah, my tree-tree...you are sick man!"

While continuing to reminisce, a somberness set in as thoughts turned to their now dead mother.

"We need to do mom proud," avowed Donald. He was always the preacher. "I stole so much shit from her that I sold to get drugs. Man, I sold her television, her stereo…she had to buy a big floor screen television so I couldn't steal it. Could you imagine me walking down the street with a big screen TV?" he laughed wholeheartedly. "Damn, I even stole a pair of her new Nike sneakers. She opened the box to wear them. She was going to walk up to Mattapan square to play her numbers and get her beer, and there was an old pair of my sneakers in there. She was heated and she knew it was me too." He laughed again.

"Yeah, we need to get off these drugs and do mom proud," Ramon stepped in to continue, "So, we are off to a new start here in Virginia Beach. We have our own place. We have our own new business. We can do this."

In unison, the three agreed that it was a new start. They guzzled down more beer as Trixie walked in front of them stooped her little cat ass down and pooped right on the brand new carpet that had been installed by the previous owner. When Stephen arrived, he arrived with three cats and no litter box. That was the first warning sign that Donald and Ramon had ignored.

Donald took a can of beer and threw it at the cat. The cat scurried out of harms way. Stephen looked at

Donald maniacally, "If you fuck with my cats, I'll kill you man."

All at once, the memories of his ways flooded the younger brothers' minds as Donald and Ramon in the same instant realized what a mistake it was to be living in the same house with him.

Chapter Forty-Six

Five months later...September 1993

Their days had become routine. Stephen would sleep on the couch all day and they went to work at night. He now had ten cats in the house still with no litter box and had just brought home a dog. On his way back from the liquor store, he had found 'Max' in a wooded area in back of their town home. His face was half gone, perhaps bitten off by some animal or maybe even shot off by a hunter. There were lots of animals in the woods of Virginia.

Stephen took Max to the veterinarian for treatment, took him home and healed him back to health. Since he took the dog in as a rescue his fees weren't that high, but he hardly had any money even for that. With half his face gone, Max was getting healthy and back on his feet. But Stephen couldn't stand the sight of him. He felt that he couldn't heal him to full health. He was tired of trying. So he took Max back to the wooded area and shot him in the head to finish the job of whatever or whoever had started.

He dug a hole and buried him.

"What happened to Max?" Ramon asked.

"He ran away," Stephen replied and never mentioned him again.

Chapter Forty-Seven

After working every night for five months, they had received very little money from Anthony, who had been collecting all receivables. He had also stolen Theresa's share of the insurance policy that was suppose to pay for their mother's funeral. So they knew he had cash. They sometimes got fifty dollars a week. When confronted, Tony said, "Well what do you think I am using to pay for your mortgage, utilities and other bills."

"Well, we should get some kind of payment for all the damn work we're doing," declared Donald taking lead for the group. He was definitely the most boisterous one.

"You do. You each get fifty dollars a week."

"So that's six hundred dollars a month for three grown ass men, who are cleaning up over thirty businesses a night. That doesn't sound right and it doesn't seem worth it."

"Don't forget, I am using my car and gas to drive you around so I'm entitled to some reimbursements. You have to pay bond insurance for the business, in case you guys decide to steal something. You have other business expenses too…"

Anthony went on and on and on. They let it pass for now. They chose not to believe their brother was stealing from *them* the money that their mother left for them to get better.

Two more months went by. It was a November, Friday morning when a note of foreclosure was posted on their door.

"What the hell is this," they yelled at Anthony when he stopped by to pick them up for work.

Ramon had finally started doing some checking. The house had been put in his name because he had completed four years in the Air Force and qualified for a VA loan. Anthony had made the first payment and that was it. He hadn't made another payment since.

"Where did all the money go?" Donald asked in disbelief anger swelling up inside him.

"What money did you think you had?" Anthony asked condescendingly.

"We have been working our asses off every day. We have over thirty accounts. We must be making some kind of money."

Tony just laughed at them and said, "There is no money. But all Ramon has to do is file bankruptcy and it will put a stop to the foreclosure and they will let you negotiate a deal, basically start all over."

They put the money issue out of their mind for yet another moment and focused on not becoming homeless. "Hey, he's our big brother. He's a real estate agent and a lawyer, so he should know what he's talking about," chimed Ramon, not believing what he himself was saying.

The bankruptcy brought them an additional three months. Yet Anthony still failed to make any payments on the property as the brothers wondered what the hell he was doing with their money they were working for each night. "What money," he would consistently tell them. We have to pay franchise fees. We have other bills and you guys keep fucking up jobs and we aren't getting paid."

He lied continuously as he simply pocketed their money while they did all the work. He figured they owed him. Donald and Ramon had stayed in his house for two months and had gotten the carpet in his guest bedroom dirty. He wanted to be paid for that and felt he deserved brand new carpet. Instead of just cleaning it, he had his entire house completely re-carpeted. He decided they owed him for much more.

In the meantime, Stephen, Donald and Ramon had numerous fights instigated by idiotic things from being high on drugs to feeling mistreated by their older brother.

Eventually, it seemed like all of Virginia Beach was after Donald. He had been selling fake drugs, stealing and running every scam he could think of to get money.

Stephen and Ramon felt like killing Donald while on a job, he would warn them, "I just want to let you know, when you get home, the TV won't be there." He would just tell them matter-of-factly every time he sold something out of their townhouse, so they wouldn't be as upset when they got home and found it to be true.

When it finally dawned on them that they were working too hard for nothing, and their belief in their brother had completely waned, they quit.

It had all hit the head of the nail when Anthony refused to send forty dollars to one of Stephen's 'girlfriends.' She was only thirteen but he directly referred to her as his girlfriend. "Quit robbing the cradle man!" they told him numerous times, "she is jail bait."

They were really shocked to hear about a little girl though. It was mostly little boys that he had been bringing to the house. He didn't seem to be harming any of them. As far as they could see, he was just taking care of little runaway boys.

In less than a year, the once new townhouse now reeked of cat urine and feces stained carpet, holes had been punched in the walls, almost all the windows had been broken. Numerous complaints were made by the neighbors to the animal society stating cruelty to animals. Ramon accidentally severed the foot of one of the cats by closing it in the sliding glass door; Stephen took the cat to the veterinarian to have him treated. The vet put a cast on the cats' leg, but the cat just kept taking it off. Again, the neighbors called the animal humane society in an attempt to get them in trouble.

With the fighting, the cat stench and the loud music, the neighbors started a petition to get them out of their subdivision. The boys were shocked when even their next door neighbor had signed the petition. He hung out, drinking and partying with them almost every day.

Stephen amidst the disgusting smell and reckless décor of the town home had started bringing home run away kids. He would nurture them, feed them and take care of them. And though neither Ramon nor Donald witnessed the actual sexual molesting of the kids, they suspected it was going on. He never bought home a kid that was older than thirteen. He had become particularly fond of one little girl that he was actually calling his girlfriend.

Ramon questioned him about all the kids he had brought into the house and had sleeping in his bedroom with him. He called him a molester. Stephen was offended. "A molester is someone who hurts kids. I love these kids." "What you are doing is molesting them idiot," Ramon said talking to him like he wasn't just stupid but plain crazy.

Appalled at the accusation, with one instant karate move, Stephen grabbed Ramon and threw him down the stairs. Ramon lay motionless at the bottom. Both Stephen and Donald thought he had killed him. They ran down the stairs to check on him and couldn't wake him up. An ambulance was called they took him to the hospital. He had a concussion and was kept overnight for observation.

Donald was extremely angry and tired. He was sick of the cats and this crazy ass fool just tried to kill his own brother because he was confronted about actually molesting children. Donald also knew Ronald was actually molesting the kids, because he had moments when he joined in with him when they lived in Syracuse. It wasn't something Donald did regularly; he blamed the drugs because he was actually disgusted by the thought of these kids being hurt. He just figured it was Stephen's world and let him live it.

But soon after doing a few rocks of crack, Donald was ready for revenge. Ramon was his full brother. They had the same father, while Anthony, Stephen and Theresa had their own dad. He had to do something to get back at him for injuring Ramon.

He knew he couldn't kick Stephen's ass. Then suddenly a great idea for revenge came to mind. "I'm gonna get rid of that damn Trixie. She's the cat who keeps having these babies and why we have all these damn cats in this nasty ass smelling place."

Stephen wasn't home when Donald put Trixie in a thick plastic lawn trash bag. He decided he would drown her. He walked at least five miles down the road into the woods off the freeway to a nearby pond off Indian Creek carrying the plastic bag over his shoulder.

But when he got to the pond he felt that it would be too cruel and decided it wouldn't be as monstrous of him to just let the cat suffocate in the trash bag instead. He took the bag, made sure it was secure, swung it in circles in the air and threw it into someone's backyard.

"Bye, bye Trixie," he yelled as he hurled the bag into the air and over the fence. He didn't watch it land as he took off running back, heading back to their house.

It took two days before Stephen noticed that he hadn't seen Trixie. Sometimes she would go off for the day but never that long. He didn't suspect foul play and Donald played sympathetic to his loss.

For two entire weeks Stephen walked around looking and yelling for Trixie.

"Trixie! Trixie!" he would call out sadly.

Donald really felt sorry for him as he watched him actually crying over the damn cat but he had avenged his brother so he continued to play the innocent and act like he was looking for Trixie sometimes.

Stephen put up flyers and just as he finally concluded that Trixie wasn't coming back, to his and particularly to Donald's surprise, Trixie walked right through the front door. Stephen was jubilant. Donald stared at Trixie astonished, but all he could do was laugh.

"You've got to be kidding me. Shit this cat must have used more than nine lives to get back here," he thought to himself. But Trixie was back, a little thinner, but otherwise the same and so the cat trend continued.

It wasn't until a month later that Stephen became suspicious of Donald.

"It was you, wasn't it?" he asked Donald, unexpectedly, the question seeming appearing out of thin air.

"What are you talking about?"

"Trixie, you tried to get rid of Trixie," Stephen accused.

"I didn't touch your damn cat!" Donald lied defensively.

"Yeah, yeah…I better not ever find out it was you." He admonished threateningly.

"Yeah, yeah, yeah, get the fuck out of here. I didn't do anything to your damn cat," Donald held in his laughter.

Chapter Forty-Eight

Donald and Ramon decided it was time to get out of Virginia and head back to Boston and leave Stephen with those damn cats of his. The health department had condemned their town home and it had been foreclosed on. They had been sneaking in at night for a place to sleep. Anthony had just said to hell with them and moved him and his family to Florida with all the money he made off of them.

On their final night together, Donald, Ramon and Stephen sat around drinking beer, smoking crack and talking trash. They decided to call their sister Theresa to let her know their brother Tony got her insurance money and that their mother's funeral had never been paid for. They told her to be glad she didn't make the mistake of coming with them. Stephen got on the phone and told her, "I should come out there to live with you. I should have listened to you. I know you were looking out for me when you told me not to go and live with them in Virginia. But after mummy died, I thought we should all be a family."

Theresa just held the phone listening to them as they told her numerous stories. She could tell they were high but also knew a lot of what they were telling her was true. She was about to move back to California. She had gone through the hell of fighting for what their mother had left them, with her biggest rival being Anthony who continuously made the claim that she made their mother change her Will.

They forgot they had told her before about his keeping the money from the insurance proceeds. The insurance company blamed the funeral home and there was no way she would get the money back.

When they hung up, they started talking about jail and how if they were in jail, they couldn't be 'got'.

"Nah man, if I was in jail, no man could get me," bragged Ramon, "but I ain't never been in jail and don't plan on going. You both have already been in, so I guess you've already been got," he laughed.

"Well let's just show him how easy it would be for someone to hold him down," Donald said lunging towards Ramon.

They playfully grabbed him and wrestled him to the ground at first unable to position him so that his ass aimed towards them. Finally they pinned him down and while Donald held him down, Stephen pulled down Ramon's pants. Ramon struggled hard to get out of their grip, which made Donald hold him down harder...until suddenly Donald heard heavy breathing coming from behind him and looked at Stephen. After getting Ramon's pants down, Stephen with his other hand had pulled down his own pants and had his dick out, erect and ready to pummel it right into Ramon's ass. As soon as Stephen saw Ramon's ass, the memories of wiping it when he had two broken arms came flooding through and he got an instant hard on and lost control of himself.

"What the hell...Are you kidding me!?" Donald yelled noticing what Stephen was about to do. He released his grip on Ramon.

"Don't let him go you stupid ass...Let me get him!" Stephen screamed at Donald angrily as he began losing his grip.

"You gotta be fucking kidding me!" Donald exclaimed again. "You're out of your damn mind. You were about to rape your own goddamn brother!"

"I was just kidding," Stephen said laughing without a flinch of guilt, "I wasn't going to do anything to him for real."

Ramon and Donald both knew he was capable and was surely about to. It was hard to fathom that he was that out of control and would actually rape his own brother. They were glad to be leaving in the morning.

When they awoke the following morning, Donald and Ramon didn't even say goodbye. They kicked a couple of his cats and left. Donald snuck in the window of their neighbor John's house and found John's car keys, stole John's car and he and Ramon drove back to Boston.

Anthony and his family had moved to Florida two months prior to their departure. Ramon and Donald went back to Boston to live in 21 Cookson Terrace which was a part of their inheritance. Theresa moved back to California from Atlanta.

Stephen continued to sneak into the town home until he could no longer get in. Homeless, he wandered the streets of Virginia Beach and finally settled down under a bridge.

For two months Stephen lived under the bridge. He lived throughout continuous rainy weather making cardboard shelters for himself and his cats. Yes, the cats...he *still* had his cats.

"If anything, we should have killed Anthony. He took all of our money while we did all the work. He was living in a nice big ass house. He had plush new carpet put down, and we end up homeless. Things would have been different if he didn't screw us over." – Stephen aka the Man in the Woods

Chapter Forty-Nine

The Woods – 1996

Tired of living under the bridge, Stephen felt abandoned, lonely and had no where to go.

"I should have listened to my sister," he stated to himself. "She warned me to stay away from them, to keep the life I had."

But he knew he had no choice but to make a change. He was making simple mistakes with the kids in Syracuse. It had been time to move. He was on the brink of being caught. Some of the kids were beginning to talk. One of the girls had caught syphilis. When Cheryl had given it to him, he had passed it on to a little girl who began forming sores in her mouth. The authorities had started an investigation to find out who molested this adorable little girl. She would have turned him in eventually.

The timing was opportune for him and he had relished the idea of being part of his family. He always felt like an outsider. But there was no way he anticipated living in Virginia Beach alone. Every one of them had deserted him.

Stephen was use to the struggle. Home for him was wherever he made it. Virginia Beach housed a lot of vacant land and there was plenty of space for him.

He combed the area until he came upon some deserted woods. There was an old shack amongst all the desolation. He decided to set up a home there. Squatting was a very common occurrence these days and this was a perfect abundance of acreage for him to claim.

There was no running water, no electricity nor any of the basic necessities. But it was shelter. He knew how to survive without those things. He didn't need very much. But he did need food. He found a bike and when it was in working condition, he used it to go to the grocery store.

With no money, he would simply steal food. But after three months of stealing his luck ran out when he was caught shoplifting two steaks and some cat food at Wal-Marts. He was arrested and incarcerated for theft.

After being ridiculed by the judge, "Mr. Gonsalves, you are a grown man. You are too old for this," he was given a light sentence. They kept him in the county jail for three months.

It was during that conviction that his brother Donald had killed their brother Ramon. They refused to release Stephen for his brother's funeral. The situation depressed him. "All because of a damn steak, I couldn't say goodbye to my brother." He requested to see the county jail's pastor.

Pastor Venable was a humbling man but he loved the Lord and enjoyed doing the Lord's work. His wife Carol was very active in the right to life organizations. She abhorred the violence of the anti-abortion fanatics and stood steadfast against it. Pastor Joe Venable was a tall sleek white man with a balding egg shaped head. Most people likened him to the Egghead character from the 1960 Batman series. But he also had smiling eyes which gave him a friendly, approachable look. He had a son that was heading quickly into his teens who was slipping from his father's reign.

Stephen liked Pastor Venable instantly and it was reciprocated. The Pastor offered to help him get a job and tried to get him an early release on good behavior, but they said his sentence was light he would serve it in full. Pastor

Venable was there to pick him up upon his release a month later.

He called his sister to check in, to let her know he was still alive and living in the woods and to find out what happened to Ramon. "I knew something was going to happen between them eventually," he told her, "they were always fighting. I can't forgive Donald though. He killed our brother. I didn't even get to say good-bye. How did he kill him?"

"Well Ramon and Donald were living in 21 Cookson Terrace. I couldn't imagine their living there because there was no running water, no electricity. They had sold all the copper piping that had been in the house to buy drugs with. They were living off of Donald's disability checks mostly and Ramon didn't like that Donald was in control.

"Why was Donald getting disability?" Stephen interrupted.

"Well," Theresa continued with a laugh, "He filed for mental reasons and after the Judge reviewed his case, he was denied. Donald got upset, jumped up and told the Judge "You must be out of your motha' fucking mind," and with that the judge then said, *'yeah there is something definitely wrong with this person, give him the disability.'*

They both enjoyed a good laugh from that.

"The outside of the house still looked great with the exception of the windows being boarded up from when Donald lit the house on fire."

"Ramon had been coming home drunk from hanging out with his friends and the two of them were getting into fights every day. Well, on the night of July 30, 1996, Ramon came home, once again drunk. Donald was in the kitchen at Cookson on top of that orange countertop high as hell. Ramon came in with a stick and just started hitting him in the head. Donald drunk a pint of Vodka that day and did about a hundred dollars worth of crack cocaine. He was pretty fucked up. The hit caught Donald off guard and he grabbed a knife off the countertop and stabbed him. He wasn't actually trying to kill him. Ramon ran outside through the back kitchen door, the knife sticking in his heart. He collapsed on the side of the house. Donald ran out after him, saw that he wasn't moving, told him to quit playing... 'Get up!' Donald yelled at him. When he realized Ramon wasn't getting up, he tried to pull the knife out of him, but it was too late. Ramon was dead."

Theresa took a deep breath and continued. "After I got the call, I got on a plane and flew out there and went straight to the county jail where they had him in downtown Boston. I took Mychal in with me. He was only five years old then. Everyone thought he was too young, but I hoped it would steer him away from drugs in the future if he could actually see the impact of what drugs could do to a person.

We took an elevator to the eleventh floor. They sat us in this little booth and then brought Donald in. There was a really thick glass between us. Donald was all beaten up. He had a huge lump on his head. He had a black eye. He was dazed and completely out of it. He sure didn't seem like the same kid we called 'Bibby' all our lives. He was talking all kind of craziness. You could see he was in mental anguish. I was told they gave him an anti-depressant which they shouldn't have because they didn't know what drug he was high on."

"Mychal asked, 'What's wrong with him and why can't we give him a hug?' I told him that is what happens when you do drugs. You aren't the same person." She paused to hold back her emotions. "The Boston Globe got the story wrong too. First they called them twins and then they likened them to Cain and Abel as if Ramon was a true saint. I called the reporter to tell her they were not twins and that perhaps if they spoke to someone in our family they would get the real story. They didn't care one bit. But then that's the media. Anyway, that's the gist of it all. Donald didn't really kill Ramon intentionally."

"Yeah, well that sounds about right, but I won't ever forgive him. He killed our brother Theresa," Stephen said with apparent sorrow. "He killed our brother."

"I just thank God that mummy wasn't here to witness it," was all she could respond.

Chapter Fifty

When Stephen went back to his place in the woods, everything was still in the same position except Carlos was now gone. He hadn't really expected the kid to still be there, but he had hoped.

He had been living in the woods of Virginia Beach for years. He rode a bike to work receiving a small stipend as a janitor at Tidewater Community College. He went to church every Sunday but the Church unaware of what was really going on encouraged his interaction with the kids. The kids helped him build his shacks in the woods; they stole food for him and brought him blankets.

His bathing place was the fountain in front of the Konikoff Professional Center located at the corner of Lynnhaven and Salem. The water pressure was great and he ducked if a police car came by. He bathed there during the midnight hours at least three times a week on his way home from work as he headed back into the woods.

After a few months the owner of the property, the Montgomery's, a wealthy couple who bred horses and owned over one hundred acres of land, noticed there was a man living on their property. With a shot gun in hand they walked out to see who he was. First they pretended to be detectives. But upon determining he was harmless and could possibly keep other squatters from living on their land and since Stephen wasn't bothering anyone, they wrote a letter for him giving him permission to live on their land.

Stephen was elated. He had a new home that he was invited to stay at. The owners also gave him miscellaneous things to add to his comfort, a small Styrofoam cooler to hold drinks in, candles, a camper cooking stove and an old bike to get around on.

Stephen was living in the woods on someone's land who was allowing it. He picked up knick knacks from neighboring garbage cans. He made beds for his cats to sleep in. He was alone and isolated from everyone. He actually liked it that way.

Chapter Fifty-One

When Stephen got locked up in the county jail where they kept short timers, Carlos had waited for three days for him to come back to the woods. He felt in his heart Stephen wouldn't outright abandon him so he figured something must have happened to him. When his hunger started getting to him, he decided he had to go out to get some food. He would stay there alone until Stephen came back. Carlos was certain he would come back to get him.

But Carlos wasn't as adept in the stealing department and on his second attempt at stealing food he was caught and put in Tidewater Detention Center. After discovering he was a little boy who was being searched for by the SVU, he was immediately sent home to his mother and stepfather.

It had been a quiet ride back to the house. Carlos was distraught when his parents pulled up to their house with him in the back seat of their platinum blue BMW convertible. Though a luxurious home, he preferred the woods.

His room was the same as he had left it. It was decorated with a redwood shaded captains bed. His large comforter was really thick and fluffy in a dark blue shade. His mother had painted his walls light blue with caricatures of skateboarders, extreme bike riders and racing cars. Things she thought he was really into. A Dell computer with a twenty-four inch monitor that acted as his television as well, sat atop his student desk. His private bathroom exited to the right of his bed. The first thing he did was take a long hot shower. He knew food would not be coming his way. While they gave him lots of material things, they only gave him food if they felt he deserved it.

His parents didn't act any different than they normally did when he was at home with them. Oh sure, they put up a façade at the police station.

"Oh, my God, my baby," his mother, Anna had cried with exhilaration, the sugar pouring sickeningly from her voice as she started kissing him all over. Carlos almost wanted to believe she truly cared until he looked over and saw his stepfather, Neil, standing by her side, arms folded, white cotton button down shirt, looking like a calm sensitive businessman. One would never imagine this conservative looking man was a child molester.

The abuse began two nights after he returned home. It was as if no time had passed. But Carlos was no longer going to tolerate it. He was tired.

He waited until his mother and stepfather fell asleep. He walked into their bedroom and kissed his mother on the forehead. Somehow he felt she had loved him. Carlos sat Indian style, legs crossed, at the edge of their king sized bed facing them. He sat there, eyes wide open, barely blinking, staring straight at them. The silky yellow sheer curtains that hung from the picture window, swayed gently from the blowing fan of the air conditioner.

After sensing someone in the room, Neil awakened after about twenty minutes. He immediately spotted Carlos. "Hey, Carlos what are you doing in here?" Neil whispered quietly, sitting up. Still staring at him, Carlos slowly lifted the gun, aiming it directly at him. His mother shifted in the bed. She hadn't awakened. Neil sat perfectly still, unsure, but daring. "Put that gun down you little shit… You are too much of a punk to use it," he said with a sneer as he put his hand out to reach for the gun. But before he could say another word, Carlos, with his small right hand, brought the trigger back and released it, shooting Neil right between his eyes. The loud noise startled his mother awake instantly. Terror arose in her as she took in the gory scene of her husband's face having been shot off. She screamed loudly. She looked at Carlos as if he were a monster. Carlos wanted to run into her arms and beg her forgiveness. He wanted to ask her if they could go back to the way things were before his daddy died. Instead, knowing that she would make sure he would never be free again, she would never tell the truth; he pulled the trigger back again and shot his mother directly in her chest killing her instantly as well.

Stephen had taught Carlos how to shoot a dangerous snake right between the eyes. He silently thanked him.

With blood and brain tissue matter all over him, he sat and waited in a trancelike state until the police arrived. He stared in the darkness of the room, thinking of the desecrated bodies simply as road kill. He anticipated that with the loudness of the gunshots along with his mother's screams that some neighbor would call the police.

Chapter Fifty-Two

When the police arrived, they found Carlos in the same position. Once they found a kid was involved, the case was turned over to the Virginia Police Special Victims Unit. Detective Young got the case. He knew the address and he was familiar with the family name. It was the home of the same boy he had been looking for earlier that year. The boy they thought was with the man in the woods. Although he had never seen Carlos in person, he recognized him immediately.

Carlos' parents had seemed like the most loving, caring parents he had met in a long time. They had seemed really concerned about the boy. He had felt extremely terrible that their kid was missing. But what a great act it had been and Detective Young had bought right into it.

After listening to Carlos' story of continuous abuse since he was five. Detective Young along with the SVU psychologist, Dr. Agnacio, questioned him on where he had been for the last seven months.

"I was just sleeping in the park mostly," he said in a quiet whisper they could barely hear.

"Your parents said you were with a man named Stephen in the woods."

Carlos looked at him with surprise, "What man?" he asked.

"Never mind. That is who your parents thought you were with," Detective Young told him with sensitivity as his voice trailed off to make the kid forget that he had asked.

"No…I never lived in any woods," Carlos lied, continuing to speak softly staring straight ahead, trying to appear in a traumatized state. His muscles went rigid. Detective Young thought it was because the boy was distressed. On the streets, Carlos had learned to respond in a stupefied manner. He felt it had been the most opportune time to use that lesson.

Detective Young was horrified at what he had heard from the kid. The damn kid was just twelve years old. The medical examiner confirmed the boys physical condition showed he had been abused for numerous years. SVU child psychologist said the kid had reached a breaking point after the system sent him back to the same conditions he had escaped from. She felt Carlos could be saved.

Detective Young decided there were mitigating circumstances and recommended to the Board of Juvenile Justice that he get sent to a Juvenile Detention Center and get daily psychiatric treatment instead. He didn't belong in jail. "For Gods sake, he's just twelve years old," was all the detective could think. "Hopefully he will be able to overcome this and he can live a normal life when he gets out. At least that man in the woods was really harmless after all," Detective Young surmised to himself.

Chapter Fifty-Three

2000 – The Millennium

Stephen was forty-four years old. His looks really hadn't changed significantly. Other than unflattering sagging jowls revealing signs of aging, he remained a light skinned black man with a yellow tone that gave him a jaundiced look. On his round head twisted, curly hair nested. Clear skin behind uncommon dark brown freckles covered his face. Hair under his chin glared like the remnants of a scar caused by a blade sliding across ones throat. Large thick bags under his eyelids were the source of his squinty eyes. Thin girlish lips accompanied a small smile. He was five feet ten inches tall, unshaven. A fat stomach hung over the same jeans he wore every day.

When the land Stephen was living on began selling off, he found solace on a neighboring property. He walked around to numerous houses knocking on the doors asking whoever answered, "Can I live with you?"

Though the city of Virginia Beach was in the current era, there still exists a large naïve community of people who desired to keep living the small town country dream. And although a stranger, when Stephen knocked on their door, most people simply opened the door, answered him cordially and continued smiling when he made such a ridiculous request.

Stephen knocked on neighboring doors until he came upon Mike and Bobbie Soulis. This time he didn't ask them if he could live with them. Instead he asked if he could live on their land, in their woods. Much to his surprise they said yes.

Bobbie and Mike owned twenty acres of land. Having him on their land would help keep the kids from trespassing. They didn't mind the kids playing in the woods until they embarked on becoming little fire bugs.

Stephen set up a tent by a small pond which was over one hundred yards from the Soulis' residence but still on their property. Bass and Bluegill fish, neighbored with various species of frogs and turtles, made the pond their home.

Stephen had to start all over. He built his place from a hood of an old car, some cardboard and anything else he could find that was useful. Again he found old bikes in the trash that he fixed and used to get to and from work. But one thing the Soulis' didn't expect ... the kids were more drawn to Stephen than anything else.

Chapter Fifty-Four

Justin was eight years old when he and his friends were playing in the woods and stumbled upon Stephen's tent. It was a pleasant Saturday afternoon.

"Hey Mister, what are you doing here?" Justin asked him with innocent curiosity. Justin appeared to be a mixture of Puerto Rican and White with a creamy skin color. He was very scrawny but the quintessence of cute. Though his brown, girlish, wide eyes drew a lot of attention to him whenever his mom took him anywhere, his shoulder length wavy hair that matched the color of his eyes, was also a great appeal. He stood there curiously with long khaki pants, a spider man t-shirt and an almost brand new pair of Keds.

The other kids, Jason and Gil didn't matter to Stephen. He was only seeing Justin. Though not always particular, Stephen had mostly been attracted to Latin children. They were more like me he reasoned being that he was considered Portuguese and Black.

"I live here," Stephen responded sheepishly.

"How can someone live out here?" asked Gil, annoyed.

"Well you see he has a tent," countered Justin.

"Yeah, well what the hell do you do out here?" Gil questioned his tone indicative of how most of the kids in the neighborhood grew up. Gil was the trouble maker of the trio.

"Not much," Stephen told them, "I just relax, go fishing, feed the animals … whatever." He spoke gently so the kids wouldn't become fearful of him.

"Well we better get going," piped in Jason. He was getting bored and he felt Stephen's eyes were beady and menacing.

"Come back again one day and I'll take you fishing." Stephen told them with anticipation.

The kids headed back in the same direction they came from.

"That man is crazy," declared Gil, giving his opinion.

"Well, he seemed kind of nice to me," said Justin, "I wouldn't mind going fishing."

"Well, I'm with Gil," confirmed Jason, "He seems a little nuts to me." They all started laughing and ran back through the woods to their homes.

Chapter Fifty-Five

It was the end of the summer, the kids continued to come over and hang out with Stephen. They all concluded he was harmless. They enjoyed hanging out with him. Justin was stealing liquor from his house to bring so they could sit around and drink with him. Justin's mother owned a tavern and she stored a lot of alcohol in their basement. And being that she drank so much she barely noticed the missing bottles.

The Soulis' no longer called the police on them because the kids had stopped lighting fires. They had promised Stephen they wouldn't start any more.

Early Saturday afternoon during the three day Columbus Holiday weekend, Stephen went to Justin's house and knocked on the door. Justin's family was very wealthy. Their home was colonial style. It was the kind of house that reminded you of a mansion where the slave owners lived in the south, complete with columns and a long front porch. His mother answered the door with a drink in her hand. Stephen could smell the alcohol.

"Hello is Justin home?"

"Who the hell are you knocking on my door, a grown man, asking for my eight year old son?" she asked stunned, her words slightly garbled.

"I'm Stephen. I came to take Justin fishing."

"Oh. Yeah. He mentioned something about that. You live in a tent on the Soulis property right? He said you were a great guy. Can I get you a drink?"

"No thank you?" Stephen replied.

"Great. I will get Justin for you," she said smiling flirtatiously. She turned around and stumbled.. "Justin!" she yelled towards the stairs. "Ah … get your fishing pole. Your friend is here to take you fishing."

Justin came darting down the stairway. He had put his fishing pole at the door the night before.

"He doesn't have a father," his mother whispered to Stephen but loud enough for Justin to hear.

"Shut up mother," he said under his breath and then quickly said aloud, "I'll see you when I get back." All her drinking annoyed him. She drank every single day.

That day on the fishing trip, Justin became yet and still another victim whose stomach was planted with weeds.

"Yeah Justin...I started with him when he was seven. He's fourteen now. He's a spoiled punk ass kid. Get's beat up in school all the time cause he can't even fight .I tried to teach him how. He's still my boy toy. He doesn't do anything except sell weed. His mother died from alcohol abuse. I saw his sister in the store the other day. I use to try to get her too. I use to chase her through the woods. She hates me." – Stephen (Sept 2007)

Chapter Fifty-Six

Las Vegas, October 2005

Theresa picked up her cell phone and pressed the talk button to answer it. The caller id identified the call as coming from Virginia. She new exactly who was calling.

"Hello," she answered nervous and unsure.

"Ms. Gonsalves this is Detective Paulson from Special Victims Unit in Virginia Beach. We got a message that you wanted to report a child molester in the Virginia Beach area."

"Yes," she responded, "I would like to report my brother has been molesting children, mostly little boys for the past twenty-five years." She could barely say the words; Stephen after all was still her brother.

"Oh really? Where does he live?" he asked curiously.

"He lives in the woods, some woods in Virginia Beach."

"Well there are lots of woods out here? Do you have a specific location?"

"No."

"How did you get this information?"

"He told me," Theresa answered.

"What made him tell you?"

"Well, I'm an author and I was trying to come up with an idea for a new book and one night when we were talking on the phone, I jokingly said I should write about his living in the woods. That jolted my memory to back when my aunt had called me and told me that my brother had kidnapped some kid and that he was in love with him. So I asked my brother to tell me about what had actually happened back then."

"How do you know he wasn't making it up?"

Theresa was at first baffled and confused by his question. "Well, I grew up with him. He was always crazy and I was actually afraid of his doing something to me. Besides that he gave me too many details and in 1996 when the FBI and the police had searched a shack he was hiding a kid in, he was really scared and nervous about being caught so he wouldn't even talk to me over the phone fearing it could have been tapped. When they searched the place, they didn't find the kid. He told me the kid hid under some floor boards or something."

"Do you know any of the victims' names?"

"No, he wouldn't give me any names…"

"Well, unfortunately there isn't anything we can do about it. You are not a victim. You can't file a complaint."

"So, basically you are telling me there is nothing you can do?"

"No, there isn't. But we will keep his name on file. What's his name?"

"Stephen," she responded faltering with fear and trepidation over the fact that she was giving up someone in her family. Not just anyone, her brother, "Stephen Gonsalves."

"You're not going to use my name in your book are you?" the officer continued seemingly more concerned about that than the kids who were being molested.

"I wasn't exactly planning on it," she responded with annoyance and condescension.

She hung up the phone angry and irritated. It had taken a lot out of her to call the police to turn her brother in. Then this pompous ass detective *hadn't* believed a word she said. She imagined he just balled up the notes he had taken and threw the paper in the trash can as if aiming at a basketball hoop.

"Thanks for nothing Detective Paulson," she said aloud to herself, as she kicked a book across her bedroom floor.

Chapter Fifty-Seven

Virginia Beach, 2005

The Rainbow Cactus was a gay men's bar which offered a lot of fun. It was a very entertaining bar with eccentric events like dinner and a movie, Ameri-queen Idol, and even line-dancing!

Half of the club is country western, half is dance music. A rainbow flag waved freely below the USA flag and welcomed you in. The word 'Cactus' over the front entrance had each letter lighted with a different color of the rainbow and when you walk in you can't help but see the bar room was also full of lights very much like a kaleidoscope. A big Soul Train disco ball floated over the dance floor. Velvet seats encircled the table.

Timmy was looking for Stephen. He would drive to Virginia Beach on the weekends from Richmond after finding out Stephen ironically was just a town away from him. After a day of searching, he would go and hang out at the Cactus.

In early 2005, amidst Michael Jackson's woes, VH1 presented the special, The Childhood Secrets of Michael Jackson. Timmy was surprised to hear about a girl named Theresa Gonsalves. He was sure she was Stephen's sister.

He had remembered a story Stephen had told him about how his sister loved Michael Jackson and had flown to Las Vegas to meet him for her sixteenth birthday. He hadn't quite known how to spell Stephen's last name but there it was right in front of him on his TV screen.

Instantly, Timmy had gone to his computer and did a search for her name and found out the information he needed. She had written a book and the information he found, led him to believe that Stephen was astonishingly just a city away in the same state.

Timmy considered calling Stephen's sister, but what would he say to her, "Hi Theresa, my name is Timmy. Your brother was like my dad when I was little but he also constantly molested me, but I was use to it and didn't mind and now I want to find him." He found himself laughing hysterically, simply at the notion.

So for months now he had been searching Virginia Beach looking for Stephen. And during his search he found the Rainbow Cactus. Timmy loved the Rainbow Cactus, especially the Ameri-Queen Idol. He had won three times. On some occasions he dressed in drag. He loved letting out his flaming side and at the Rainbow Cactus, he knew he wouldn't run into any of his co-workers in there. But on a few occasions he saw this cute little guy that he desperately wanted to meet.

Chapter Fifty-Eight

Carlos was released from the juvenile detention center when he turned nineteen. He had been there for seven long years. He had faired better off than most of the kids, because for him, being there was easier than to have continued being abused by his parents. And it was definitely a greater alternative than life in prison.

He felt no remorse at killing his parents. He wondered if love existed in his heart. He knew he felt love when he was with Stephen and wondered if he would again. He started looking for Stephen as soon as he was released.

But Carlos wasn't free from the haunting of murdering his parents. For the past seven years he had vicious nightmares about them. He dreamt of them and Stephen constantly. In his dreams his feelings were pure and apparent. When he dreamt of his parents the hatred was untainted. When he dreamt of Stephen, his longings for his hugs were real.

He got a job working at Kroger's Grocery store. It wasn't paying enough money so he would also prostitute himself to live the high life style he so eagerly preferred. Most of his clientele were from Fredericksburg, VA so no one where he lived would suspect what he was doing. To everyone else he was simply a bag boy at Kroger's making $6.50 per hour. When he was released from the youth facility, he also received one hundred thousand dollars from his mother's life insurance policy. As he wondered where all the other money had gone, he decided to use the money to purchase a small house which he decorated nicely.

He got a small dog from a Kroger patron who was giving them away. The dog, a male, Carlos named Jasper was a gold and white Shitzu, with a royal stride along with an extreme overbite. It was the overbite that kept him from being a show dog. With Carlos and Jasper love was imminent. Jasper made coming home a joy as he greeted him happily each day with a small pillow he would carry in his mouth as if to give Carlos a gift.

To escape from his real every day life, he would often hang out at The Rainbow Cactus, a gay bar on

Holland Road. He loved to dance and at the Rainbow Cactus he could line dance and also get funky. He loved it. He had noticed this one really handsome guy who sometimes dressed in drag had been eyeing him on his last two visits and wondered when he was going to come over and ask him to dance.

To his surprise, when he returned from a run to the bathroom, a fresh drink sat on his table top. He turned and looked around for the handsome stranger, hoping it had been from him, but the lights hindered him from seeing and the disappointment on his face was obvious. He turned around to take his seat and there stood the stranger with a bright smile.

"Hi, I'm Timothy Allen, but my friends call me Timmy," he said extending his hand smoothly and with refinement.

"Well, hey now!" Carlos said sweetly however nervously, "I am Carlos Diaz. Is this drink from you?" he asked his voice now an almost quiver. He was shocked at himself for feeling so nervous and wondering what prompted it, as his eyes fluttered flirtatiously. Could it be love at first sight? He had to calm himself down.

"Yes, that drink is from me. Is it alright if I sit with you? Or would you like to dance?" Timmy found himself calm but unusually drawn to this Carlos kid. He knew Carlos had to be at least twenty-one to get in the club. And because the club was a gay bar, often being harassed by the enforcement agencies who tried to close them down, the Rainbow Cactus was very strict on checking identification.

"We can save the dancing for later, let's sit for awhile. Let's just talk," Carlos spoke quickly.

Timmy and Carlos both sat down each feeling a familiarity with each other. They made small talk and touched base a little on their early childhoods but with no grand information. When the comfort level grew between them, they danced and played a little pool.

Timmy felt Carlos was somewhat fragile and a bit insecure so he decided to not try to rush into anything with him, at least not on the first night. He smiled within.

From that first evening together, their relationship spiraled into an instant love affair. Timmy was the stronger of the two, the caregiver, who enjoyed taking care of Carlos. When the commitment was secure, Carlos quit his side job as a gigolo and their relationship became strictly monogamous and Carlos asked Timmy to move into his house with him.

Chapter Fifty-Nine

Carlos and Timmy's relationship was special. Carlos felt like a little kid and Timmy took care of him. Whether it was financially, physically or emotionally, he was there for Carlos.

Carlos often had severe nightmares. He would awaken in sweat, often soaked. It was after one of these nightmares as Timmy held Carlos rocking him in his arms that Carlos revealed everything to him.

"My step-dad did stuff to me!" he cried, "and my mother allowed it. And when I was twelve I just lost my mind. I couldn't take it any more and I killed them."

Timmy was shocked at first, but he understood being a victim of abuse and sometimes the weaker ones flipped out.

"I had run away from home and I was living in the woods with this man named Stephen and he took really good care of me and then he went missing and I got sent back home. Stephen was the closest thing to a real father I ever had. He really loved me. I had to please him too, but I didn't mind because he really truly loved me. He played with me. He took me fishing, to the movies. I have been trying to find him since I was released and I don't know where he is. When I got out of the youth facility after seven years, the woods had been turned into new houses and office buildings, so I really don't know where to begin searching now."

"That's strange," said Timmy scratching his head, "I am looking for a guy named Stephen who was like a father to me when I was six or seven. My mother was hooked on drugs. She didn't care about me. Well, I should say the drugs were more important to her. Stephen had been my day care teacher, but my mom left me with him all the time. He did the same things for me…clothed me nicely, bought me new shoes, always took me fishing and to movies. And yes, I had to do what he asked, but I didn't mind, well I did, but I endured it because he was giving me what I really needed at the time. Love."

Timmy and Carlos looked at each other. Could it be the same man they wondered to themselves in bewilderment?

"What's his last name?" Timmy asked and at the same time they both said "Gonsalves."

"Wow!" exclaimed Carlos, "this is uncanny. No way. How did you know to come here to Virginia Beach?"

"Well I ended up in Richmond when my mom decided to ask my grandmother to help her get off of the drugs. Mom is still struggling with it, but whatever. Well one day I saw his sister, at least I believed it was his sister, on a VH1 special about Michael Jackson and I looked her up on line and found out Stephen was in Virginia Beach. I couldn't believe how close I was to him. We were in Syracuse, New York when he was taking care of me."

"Oh my God!" Carlos flailed, "now I understand why we have such a bond. I can't believe it. We have to find him."

"Yeah but how do you really feel about him. Some days I want to hug him and call him daddy. Some days I wish I could just kill him. He molested us at a young age if you look at it realistically, but on the other side of it he also saved my life," Timmy stated.

"Sometimes my nightmares are about killing him. And sometimes I just wish for my daddy Stephen." Carlos' voice was sad and reminiscent of those six months in the woods with Stephen.

They decided to continue the search together. They felt somehow that God had brought them together.

"Yeah, let's still try to find him. And if we look at him and loathe him, we can still turn him in. If we look at him and love him we'll have our daddy back." Timmy said while smiling.

Carlos smiled at the thought and then he asked jealously, "What if he has some other little kid he loves now?"

Timmy just took Carlos in his arms, holding him closer and rocked him. "We will find him."

"When Michael Jackson got caught, I decided I should stop. I figured if it was easy for him to get caught, I really will get caught. Some of the kids are older now like eighteen and want to continue the relationship. I told them they need to leave me alone. I haven't done it for about a year now. Do you think Michael is guilty Theresa? I know he is, partly because of the animals and all the toys and kid stuff he has at his house. He's just like me." – Stephen aka the Man in the Woods. (2006)

Chapter Sixty

2365 Salem Road
The Little Red Storage Shed
2005 - 2007

Another beautiful spring morning filled the sky of Virginia Beach, May, 2007 when Theresa and Illiya pulled up slowly to 2365 Salem Road. Illiya and Theresa were great friends. They had met over ten years ago in Los Angeles, California where they both worked in television and music video production.

Illiya now lived in Norfolk, neighboring city to Virginia Beach. This made Theresa's visit there a plus. Theresa made Illiya privy to the purpose of her trip and Illiya refused to allow her to go by herself. How could she let her friend go alone to visit her brother who sounded like he had the makings of a mad man? She couldn't.

The drive from Illiya's house was quick as they passed several acres of forested land. When they arrived on Salem Road, Illiya drove slowly until they reached their desired destination. From the road, there was a clear view of the home of Mike and Bobbie Soulis. They pulled into an arch shaped driveway which was separated by a nicely kept artificial pond.

The house seemed closed to the world. They noticed a partially screened in porch or sun room which was filled with junk. It appeared as if the Soulis' were hoarders. It seemed like everything they owned was in this one room. There didn't seem to be anyone at home. They sat in the driveway looking around. Numerous abandoned cars, some visible and some appearing hidden, surrounded the area.

They saw the shed that they thought Stephen lived in that was partially hidden by the large trees. It seemed a far distance from the house. Fear immobilized them. They refused to get out of the car. They heard a dog barking loudly coming from the premises but they couldn't see one. Finally, they realized that since the property was wide open if he wasn't tied up, then the dog would just run off the property.

They were only sitting there nervously for three minutes but it felt like an hour, when they finally decided to get out of the car and knock on the door. They walked carefully, almost tiptoeing, jumping at every little sound they thought out of place. Theresa knocked on the door. The dog barked again, otherwise there was complete silence. They stood there and knocked again, speaking to each other nervously about walking to the little red shed they saw in the back. As they turned to walk away, the door opened and a large dog aggressively and ferociously started barking and jumping anxiously against the side window, in attack mode. The girls jumped fearfully, feeling as if they were victims in a horror movie.

"Can I help you?" asked Bobbie Soulis.

"Uhm ...I am looking for my brother Stephen. Stephen Gonsalves. I am his sister Theresa," she responded uneasily.

"Oh my God..." Bobbie replied, her eyes watering, "I can't believe you are here. Stephen talks about you all the time. I can't believe it. Does he know you are here?"

"Ahh ... No. It's a surprise."

"Oh my God," she said again, "I have to see this. You're the only one in the family he really talks about. Let me knock on the door and tell him he has a surprise!" Bobbie was definitely more excited than Theresa could ever be.

Illiya and Theresa looked at each other questioningly with their eyes as they smelled alcohol reeking from her … "Is she drunk?"

Bobbie was about five feet tall, extremely skinny with short hair. She was wearing blue and white checkered pajama pants with a large white t-shirt while light blue slippers completed the outfit.

Bobbie almost sprinted to the little red storage shed. She knocked hard and rapidly on the door.

"Stephen, open the door. There is a big surprise for you out here. You have a visitor." Bobbie didn't wait for him to open the door she just opened it up. Theresa stuck the upper half of her body in the door as a decaying smell filled her nostrils.

Stephen lifted up out from under the covers. "Some things never change," Theresa thought to herself as she watched him. He looked at her with sleepy eyes, barely recognizing her at first glance.

"Hi Tootie, it's me! Don't act like you don't recognize me!"

"Theresa?" Stephen asked uncertain, "but then who the hell else calls me by that damn name anymore," he reflected.

"Yes, what you don't recognize me?" she chuckled.

"Wow…what are you doing here? Let me get some clothes on," he said getting out of the bed. She backed out the door and a few feet away from the shed to get some fresh air. Stephen's cat Felix followed her out the door.

Bobbie in all of her sentimental glory had started to cry. Prior to that moment, she had felt that Stephen was alone in the world and couldn't hold back happy feelings for him.

Chapter Sixty-One

Theresa and Illiya stood outside while Stephen dressed. Not even a glimpse of the sun could enter his lodging as vines covered most of the windows, blocking daylight from penetrating through.

At first glance the shed looked like a warm cozy summer cottage which simply needed a fresh coat of paint. Its warm red color was actually inviting. A small picket white fence paralleled the front door and complimented the shack giving the appearance of a glimpse into a Norman Rockwell painting. But the illusion was instantly shattered once the tall brown door opened.

Above the open doorway, old spider webs filled every crevice. Empty tuna cans, water bottles, paper plates and old newspaper covered the floor. A bed to the immediate left of the doorway was the remains of a pull out sofa bed. At the edge of the bed, a ladder of assorted furniture held a small thirteen inch color television. A tiny refrigerator sat next to it.

The place smelled rotten. Theresa couldn't tell if it was the mildew, the cat or the fact that his bathroom consisted of a bucket. Stephen occupied an eighth of the shed, if that much. The rest was filled with old materials for repairs that were never made. But it didn't seem to matter to Stephen. The small red shed was a place to live.

He had come to live there because some teenagers skipping class from the high school nearby started hanging out in the woods and began harassing him. He would threaten them but they kept a far distance to keep him from getting to them. But when he finally did catch them, still cognizant of his karate skills, he gave them each the necessary beat down they deserved.

In the midst of their anger, they waited for him to go to work one evening, crept into the woods and lit the shack afire. He vowed to get back at them somehow.

As Stephen was deciding what part of the woods he could move to where he wouldn't have to withstand the kids' constant harassment, the Soulis' offered to let him live inside the little red storage hovel that sat in back of their house where the woods began.

Mike Soulis was aware of Stephen's antics with the kids. He hadn't seen him do anything harmful to them, but Mike felt it just wasn't natural for a grown ass man to hang around in the woods with so many little boys.

After promising to fix the space into livable conditions, Mike told him he could stay there as long as he didn't bring any little boys there. They promised he would be left alone. That's all he wanted... was to be left alone. Stephen accepted. He was a little tired of all the rain that fell in the woods of Virginia. He was tired of ducking from lightening. This offer was a blessing.

Stephen enjoyed living like a hermit. He walked the streets at night as his shadow followed him through the moonlight. He continued to work his night job at the Tidewater Community College. He refused to eat out in restaurants and slept most of the day to avoid people. He just didn't want to be bothered.

He simply wanted to be alone with his cat Felix, in the small crowded shed, on the Soulis' eight acres of land, which after two years was still inhabitable.

Chapter Sixty-Two

Stephen was surprised and shocked that his sister showed up with her friend. She came knowing that he had been with the kids. *"She still loves me,"* he felt. The thought made him smile. Theresa had warned him that if he didn't call her with a date for her to visit then she would just show up. She had been true to her word.

He knew she wanted more information for her new book. He would give her a few nibbles but nothing more than that. What she wrote could destroy what little life he had. He had to get rid of her as quickly as possible. But she was the only one in the family who kept any real line of communication open with him.

He almost found himself in tears when he saw her. He didn't want to show any emotion. He hadn't seen her since their mother's funeral in 1993 and now here it was 2007. A lot of time had passed. She had put on some weight. But he himself had a pot belly from drinking beer every single day. That was his past time. Smoking weed and drinking beer. His job was still in tact he told her. And they girls laughed as he told them about getting caught at work with some weed.

"I found a big farm of weed that the kids had grown. They had burned down my shack that I use to live in and I figured I was going to get something out of it and get back at them, so I found the farm they planted. It was raining but I took some plastic bags and pulled up as much as I could. I rode my bike to work and passed by three or four cop cars and I thought each time they would stop me because the plastic bags looked suspicious. When I got to work I realized it was wet and needed to dry out and I figured I would just dry it out in the microwave." Theresa and Illiya started laughing already knowing what happened to the weed.

"Suddenly the whole entire place smelled like weed and my boss walked in. He took one sniff and said what the hell is going on in here. And I just looked at him, just knowing I was caught and I said ... Oh, I was just heating up some spinach. He just said okay and walked out of the room."

"I'm sure he really knew but he never said anything else about it. I thought he was going to get security and have me arrested."

"Then the other day he told me that I had to stop feeding the foxes and other animals in back of the school. He just looked at me and said you're not going to stop are you. I told him no. He just said okay and walked away."

Stephen knew he was babbling. He was nervous. She wanted information about the kids. He wanted her to leave. He was genuinely happy to see her but he wasn't quite ready to have his world destroyed.

Another damper, however, was put on their visit. Crazy Mike showed up ranting and raving telling Stephen he had to leave. Theresa and Illilya had dubbed him crazy Mike after hearing stories about him from Stephen. He had just been released from county lock up for domestic violence. His wife, the girls had nicknamed Drunk Ass Bobbie, wouldn't quit drinking and Crazy Mike had tried to control her life. And because Stephen hadn't backed up Mike's story to the police, Mike wanted him out.

"I want you out of here by Monday," Crazy Mike yelled at him in front of his sister whom he had never taken the time to even introduce himself to nor even venture a simple hello. Theresa was humiliated for her brother as she stood there listening to Stephen beg to stay in such a horrid place.

279

Stephen was disturbed by the incident. He asked the girls to take him to Wal-Mart so he could get a new tire pump, then he decided it was time for his sister to go. He told her he needed some sleep. She tried to get him to go out to dinner. He refused. She tried to get him to go look for an apartment. "I don't do rent," he told her.

He wasn't worried about it he told her. He may even take the story to the Fox Channel as an illegal eviction. After all, the law in Virginia states that whether he is paying rent or not, as long as he is getting mail there as his residence, he needs to be given a thirty day notice. His paychecks were mailed there every week.

Stephen walked them to the car. He was glad they were leaving. It relieved the pressure from him. If she stayed around longer he would probably break down. He had already told her too much. He actually mentioned his boy-toy in front of her friend. He hugged her, kissed her on the cheek and said he would be more in touch. He went back into his shack and jacked off at the thought of his sister. Nothing had changed in his conflicted heart.

"I have to be really good at this house. This is a real place for me to live. I can't bring any kids here or they will kick me out. He almost caught me here once when one of my boy toys came over." – Stephen aka The Man in the Woods

Chapter Sixty-Three

Tears slid down Theresa's eyes. She loathed what he had done. Hell, she had always thought he was crazy. He had ruined many, many lives. She wondered why none of the kids had come forward. Stephen was in plain site. He didn't hide behind trees or dark glasses or dark clothing. He hid behind a mask of sanity. However, when Theresa spoke to him, she always saw the disguise fall off.

Strangely, she also wanted to help him. She pitied him, but pity wasn't what he wanted. He was also too old for her to rescue. After all, he didn't think he needed rescuing. She wanted to forgive and forget what she knew about him. Somehow she knew she would never see Stephen again.

As they drove away, Theresa knew she alone could not correct the sins of their ancestors. She had to put that in God's hands and pray that the cycle within her family would be broken.

Arriving back in Las Vegas, she looked at her own son Mychal. He loved children too. Would she carry a cloud of suspicion about her own son? What about her cousins and nephews? Her heart tugged as she looked at her son's wide smile…. "No, not my Mychal," she thought, "Not in a million years."

"How's Mychal doing? If he keeps acting up, why don't you just send him out here to live me in the woods. I'll take good care of him. (He laughs)"- Stephen aka The Man in the Woods. (September, 2007)

Chapter Sixty-Four

Stephen found a new location in the woods. As was usual, there were neither roads nor trails leading to his newly claimed land. No one would ever really find him there unless he was followed. He did show Pastor Venable how to get there in case he didn't show up for work for a few days. And when in fact that did happen, Pastor Venable contacted the police.

When Detective Young heard the name he remembered the man in the woods from when they were looking for the boy, Carlos. He decided to go take a look for himself.

Pastor Venable took Detective Young to the opening leading into the woods where Stephen had shown him his latest home. His home consisted of a cheap plastic tent that he had gotten from Wal-Mart, a battery operated radio, a kerosene cooking stove, and miscellaneous things he found along the way.

When they arrived at the entrance to Stephen's neck of the woods, Detective Young instructed Pastor Venable,

"Stay here and wait for me to return. About how far in is it?"

"At least two or three miles," Pastor Venable responded.

Detective Young took a deep breath as he looked at the heavy brush that he would have to trek through.

"Two or three miles in, huh?" Young asked with a great deal of apprehension.

Joe Venable shook his head affirmatively, "Yeah, I've only been there once. You should come to a large clearing in the middle of some trees. I believe there is a small creek there. He had talked about leaving so maybe he just left, but I would appreciate it if you could just check it out."

Detective Young smiled to himself. It had been twelve years since he last ventured into the woods. He could barely make it to the location then and now once again he had to go searching through the woods regarding the same creep.

The same guy he knew actually had held Carlos captive in the woods when SVU and the FBI were looking for him. Stephen Gonsalves, the same guy who was questioned for possibly molesting Justin Tilman, whose mother suspected, was the case. But when Justin denied any such thing happened, once again they had to let him go.

As Detective Young peered into the woods, Joe could see the exasperated look on his face. "I have a bike in my truck if that would help you?" Joe offered walking towards his truck knowing the detective would need it.

"Yeah that would be great," he responded with slight gratitude, "there's no other way huh?"

Joe smiled at him as he took the bike down from the back of his pick up truck.

"Good luck!" he said handing it to him.

When perps became able to out run police officers on numerous occasions, the department demanded that all officers get on some kind of daily exercise plan.

Detective Young figured since he rode a stationary bike to get that required exercise forced upon him, this should be a breeze.

"Pastor Venable, I'll go check on your friend. If I don't come back soon, call my unit and have them send back up," he ordered. "In the meantime, let's just hope I don't have a heart attack." He smiled.

It took Detective Young almost twenty-five minutes to bicycle to the clearing Pastor Venable directed him to and let's not reveal the fact that he stopped twice because he was short of breath. "Should have quit smoking these damn cigarettes a long time ago," he said aloud knowing no one could hear him.

He stepped off the bike leaving it behind a tree. He spotted a small plastic tent and noticed it was torn to shreds. He walked towards the tent and kicked a crushed radio and a small cooking stove. "What happened here?" he wondered, thinking perhaps some animals had trampled the tent. He walked further combing the wooded areas of the clearing and then he saw him. There lay Stephen Gonsalves stuck under a large tree trunk weighting down his body. A large old tree, struck by lightening, plummeted down pinning him to the ground.

Detective Young ran over to him. Stephen was lying, wincing in obvious pain. He was fully conscious. He stared at the Detective recognizing him from years earlier when he had come looking for Carlos. He mouthed the word "HELP." Blood dripped out of numerous bites all over his face from what looked like a fox or maybe even a black bear. Three of Stephen's fingers were missing. He could still survive if Detective Young got the trunk off of him or went for help. But Detective Young's mind was somewhere else. Call it momentary insanity.

"No sense in trying to rescue him and hurting myself," thought Detective Young, "But how cruel would it be to just leave him here like this?"

Detective Young ran back to the tent area. There was nothing there that could help him lift the tree. He hadn't been looking for that. He had noticed an oil can that Stephen used for the lantern or the camper cooking stove. It gave Detective Young an idea.

He walked over to Stephen and poured the oil all over his stifled body. Detective Young took a cigarette out of his pocket, Salem low menthol. He lit it with the lighter he always carried. He stood smoking it. It took three long deep puffs to get it well lighted until a long flaming ash hung down. He took the cigarette and threw it on Stephen.

Stephen ignited instantly into a ball of flames. A howling sound erupted from deep inside him. If anyone was nearby they surely would have mistaken it for the sound of a wounded animal.

Detective Young watched the body burn until it was singed and charred beyond recognition. The woods were damp from recent rains. The fire would smolder out. When he couldn't stand the indescribable smell of burning human flesh anymore, he started out of the woods.

"Someday, someone will discover the remains. But I couldn't have been the one to get this monster help to wreak havoc on any other children," thought the detective unremorsefully.

When he arrived back, he was a little dirty and disheveled. He brushed himself off hoping the smell of scorched human garbage didn't accompany him. His breathing was heavy again.

"Well Pastor Venable," the detective said winded, "There was no one in the woods. I did see a tent that was smashed up as if abandoned and there was an old cooking stove but no signs of anyone living there for a while."

"I suppose he may have just left town. His locker was empty as well. Oh well. Maybe his sister will call again soon and I will ask her if she knows where he went. Thanks for checking," he said as Detective Young handed him the bike back. "Well, we will look around for another couple of days. He's a grown man and since his locker has been cleared out, we probably won't consider it a missing person's case." He extended his hand to the Pastor.

Pastor Joe Venable shook the detective's hand, got in his pickup truck and drove off. For some reason, he felt relieved. Maybe it was good that Stephen was gone.

Detective Young took another cigarette out of his pocket, started to light it then threw it to the curb.

The flesh of the weed planter had been turned into ash. His bones remained under the fallen tree. Stephen was where he belonged … in the ground … in the woods.

Epilogue

2007 was coming to an end. Timmy and Carlos had just celebrated Carlos' twenty-third birthday. In November Timmy had turned thirty. They had a big party celebration at the Rainbow Cactus. It was a lot of fun. When they arrived home, Carlos went straight to bed. He had been tired and a bit depressed at not having any family to share in his birthday. After Carlos was in bed, Timmy told him he was going out to get something to eat.

When Carlos drifted off into a deep sleep, he immediately fell prey to his nightmares. '*Carlos took the head and placed it next to the head of the dead deer. He wished he had a silver platter to put it on. He looked at Stephen's eyes starring up at him from the ground. Carlos was breathing very hard. He had chased Stephen for almost two miles before he caught him. He had waited for this moment since Stephen abandoned him and left him alone in their little shack twelve years ago. He had chased him with a hatchet and cut off his head. He didn't even wince from all the blood....* "*I curse the day I met you... I curse the day*

291

I met you....." *he yelled as he chopped. Then from afar out comes his stepfather, his face shot off, gut matter hanging off the sides of what was left of it. "I am coming to get you Carlos....don't you miss your dear old stepfather?" Carlos turned and started to run screaming.*

Timmy heard the screaming coming from their bedroom as he sat down stairs. He had come back over an hour ago and when he looked in on Carlos he had seemed to be sleeping peacefully. He ran up the stairs.

"Hey wake up Carlos ..." Timmy told him gently rocking him.

"It's just a dream for now, but don't worry, we will find him one day... We will find him one day for sure!"

Together they had been looking for Stephen for almost two years. Carlos still couldn't remember exactly where they had stayed in the woods. It had been too many years and he had only been twelve at the time. He had loved Stephen, even called him dad. Tears came to his eyes. He didn't really want to kill him. He still loved him. He missed him. He still wanted his daddy. They both did.

With enthusiasm and revelation in his voice, Timmy, as if suddenly remembering something announced excitedly, "I have a little birthday surprise for you. Come downstairs and I will show you." He grabbed Carlos out of the bed and nearly dragged him down the stairs and into the living room.

In the living room, there sat Walter. He was ten years old. He was *their* newest toy, *their* newest victim. The cycle had continued; they were sexually confused, their sexual abuse embedded within them for life.

Walter, with Carlos' dog Jasper on his lap, looked lovingly up at them with his big brown eyes and smiled, "Hi Daddy."

"Stephen Gonsalves, my brother, was born with morals but no conscience. You can not grow a conscience."
— Theresa J. Gonsalves

About the Author

Theresa Gonsalves was born November 24, 1958 in Boston, MA. Raised in a dream world with Michael Jackson as her savior, at the age of 12, his songs gave her life reassurance. Yet, Theresa managed to turn her fantasy to reality. With diligence, one would never imagine coming from a young girl, she flew to Las Vegas to meet Michael Jackson for her 16th birthday. This self-learned persistence and hard work makes Theresa who she is today, a woman entrepreneur, conquering life with her own company and working on future novels.

Theresa had a fervent desire to write at a young age. Her heartfelt letter writing inspired Michael Jackson to want to meet *her*. He stated her letters made him feel like she was talking directly to him. In fact, she *was* talking to him through her letters when he wrote the song Billie Jean about her!

A devastating heartbreak made Theresa sit down and write her first novel, **"OBSESSIONS"** which details how her fixation with Michael Jackson, led her to obsessive, destructive behavior. Writing was her therapy.

Theresa currently resides in Las Vegas, NV. She is single and has two sons, Mychal (17) and Todd (25).

Other Books by Theresa J. Gonsalves

OBSESSIONS (the shocking true story of the Real Billie

Jean in Michael Jackson's Life)

Check it out at Amazon.com or

www.obsessionsthebook.com

For pictures and more detail related to

THE MAN IN THE WOODS

go to

www.themaninthewoods.com

Also check out LOVE AGAINST SOCIETY by her son

Todd Love Ball Jr.

www.toddloveballjr.com

TJG Management Services, Inc., Las Vegas, NV